"I would erase those images for you if I could."

Tessa squeezed Mason's hand. "I know."

As expected, Lily was asleep when they pulled into the stables' lot and parked. Tessa suggested staying inside the truck with her, but Mason shot down that idea. They had to unload the horses, remove their gear and brush them down, not to mention dole out their overdue supper.

Tessa carried Lily inside and got comfortable in one of the break room chairs. She would've liked to help the officers, but they had a certain routine and would accomplish that faster without her underfoot. Fishing her phone from her pants pocket, she settled in to watch her favorite music videos.

At first, she didn't pay attention to the loud voices coming from deeper in the building. Then a shot rang out, a̶n̶d̶ ̶s̶h̶e̶ ̶f̶l̶i̶n̶c̶h̶e̶d̶. The door was flung open, and Mason ̶ ̶ ̶ ̶ ̶ ̶ ̶ ̶ ̶ ̶ ̶ ̶ ̶ ̶ and his eyes hard.

"Dante's m̶ ̶ ̶ ̶ ̶ ̶ ̶ ̶ ̶ ̶ ̶ ̶ aying the building w̶ ̶ ̶ ̶ ̶ ̶ ̶ ̶ ̶ ̶ n us out and pick us off, one by one."

Karen Kirst was born and raised in east Tennessee near the Great Smoky Mountains. She's a lifelong lover of books, but it wasn't until after college that she had the grand idea to write one herself. Now she divides her time between being a wife, homeschooling mom and romance writer. Her favorite pastimes are reading, visiting tearooms and watching romantic comedies.

Books by Karen Kirst

Love Inspired Suspense

Explosive Reunion
Intensive Care Crisis
Danger in the Deep
Forgotten Secrets
Targeted for Revenge

Visit the Author Profile page at Harlequin.com for more titles.

TARGETED FOR REVENGE

KAREN KIRST

LOVE INSPIRED SUSPENSE
INSPIRATIONAL ROMANCE

LOVE INSPIRED® SUSPENSE
INSPIRATIONAL ROMANCE

Recycling programs
for this product may
not exist in your area.

ISBN-13: 978-1-335-40516-6

Targeted for Revenge

Copyright © 2021 by Karen Vyskocil

This edition published by arrangement with Harlequin Books S.A.

For questions and comments about the quality of this book, please contact us at CustomerService@Harlequin.com.

Love Inspired
22 Adelaide St. West, 40th Floor
Toronto, Ontario M5H 4E3, Canada
www.Harlequin.com

Printed in U.S.A.

To appoint unto them that mourn in Zion, to give unto them beauty for ashes, the oil of joy for mourning, the garment of praise for the spirit of heaviness; that they might be called trees of righteousness, the planting of the Lord, that he might be glorified.

–Isaiah 61:3

This is dedicated to the women who took a chance
on my first book about an undercover outlaw.
Who could've guessed that would lead to a twelve-book
series? And when the historical line closed,
you let me try my hand at bombs and explosions.
Thank you to Love Inspired editors Emily Rodmell
and Tina James for guiding my publishing career.

Acknowledgments

This book wouldn't have been possible without the
invaluable insight and input from Sergeant Jeff Duren of
the Hendersonville Mounted Police Unit. Thank you, Jeff,
for your willingness to help with my fictional world. More
important, thank you for your service to the community.

Any mistakes are purely my own.

ONE

Tessa Elliott was used to looking over her shoulder. Searching crowds for that one familiar face had become a habit during the four years she'd been in hiding. But she wasn't as diligent as in the beginning, and the meaning of the librarian's remark didn't immediately register.

"A man was asking for me?" Tessa repeated, angling away from the children seated on the patterned carpet. "Did he give you his name?"

"No, I'm afraid not. He looked like a visitor from Atlanta," she said. "He was dressed in a three-piece suit. His accent wasn't local, though."

Dread congealed in her stomach. "Did he have black hair? And a scar above one eyebrow?"

"Come to think of it, he did have a scar. He's awfully handsome. Polite, too. Is he a friend of yours?"

Tessa slipped on her cross-body canvas bag. "Did you tell him where I live?"

Mrs. Smith looked down her crooked nose at her. "I wouldn't do that. I did tell him you and Lily are regulars at the children's story hour."

She turned a full circle, searching the stacks for an intimidating figure she'd learned to fear from a young age. "When was he here?"

"Not long after we opened," she said. "Are you in some sort of trouble, Tessa?"

He'd been in town for three hours already? Maybe longer?

"I—I have to go." Rushing forward, she scooped Lily into her arms. Her surprised cry caused the children's librarian to halt her story and the other children to stare.

"Mommy, I want to stay!"

"We're going on an adventure, ladybug." She hurried through the double doors, only to stop and scan the parking lot and surrounding streets for hulking vehicles with blacked-out windows. There were mostly dusty pickup trucks and minivans. She dashed to her battered Toyota sedan and got Lily secured in her car seat.

"Why can't the 'venture wait until after the story?"

Tessa met her three-year-old's gaze in the rearview mirror. Dark curls formed a halo around her pale, round face.

"I know you're upset to miss story time, but this can't wait."

"I didn't get a snack."

"I'll get you one at home."

She sped through the picturesque Georgia town and prayed the Southern hospitality she'd found so comforting hadn't led Dante straight to her door. At least Mrs. Smith had had the good sense not to share her address. In her neighborhood, she drove past her rental house three times before she was satisfied it was safe to enter.

If Lily hadn't needed to use the potty, she would've left her in the car only long enough to grab the emergency travel bags she kept in her bedroom closet. Instead, she ushered her into the quiet house and deactivated the alarm. Blood surged through Tessa's veins, throbbing erratically at her neck, rushing through her ears and making her light-headed.

"We need to get on the road."

Lily did a pirouette in the hallway, her shoulder-length nut-brown curls flaring. "Where are we going?"

Tessa's throat threatened to close up. If her brother had tracked her down, she had only one choice. She must go to Lily's father, Mason Reed. "You'll see soon enough." Lightly tapping her nose, she flicked on the bathroom switch. "Hurry, okay?"

Tessa strode to the opposite side of the house, past the kitchen and into her bedroom, then jerked the bags from her closet. Over the years, she'd periodically switched out Lily's clothes for bigger sizes. The last time had been around Easter, so most of the clothes would be season-appropriate. She grabbed the accordion file from the desk, the one containing legal documents, including the birth certificate Mason had never seen or dreamed existed.

The sound of a male voice startled her. Had Dante or one of his guards somehow gotten in? She'd drilled Lily not to open the door, not for any reason.

Dropping everything, she ran to Lily's bedroom.

"I want to see you today," the man said. "Maybe at the park. What do you think, Lily?"

Lily danced around the speaker and video-surveillance apparatus. Seeing Tessa in the doorway, she grinned. "Mommy, my friend wants to see me. Can we play at the park?"

Tessa gripped the doorjamb for support and stared at the dresser, where she'd placed the popular security feature right after Christmas.

"What do you say, Mommy?" the deep, disembodied

voice mocked her, even though she'd remained out of its view. "Can we play?"

That voice had featured in her nightmares.

Dante had not only found them, but he'd also invaded their sanctuary by hacking into their security system. Battling nausea, she waved Lily over to the door. Taking her hand, she hustled her to the garage and buckled her in. Then she retrieved the bags from the hallway outside her room. As the garage door was going up, she got behind the wheel and started the engine.

"Lily, how long have you been talking to your friend?"

She bounced her pair of sparkly stuffed ponies through the air, completely unaware of the tension in Tessa. "Don't know."

"Since Christmas?"

She shook her head.

"Easter?"

"Uh-uh."

Tessa gave up. How long her Mafia prince of a brother had been in contact with her daughter wasn't the point. The car screeched out of the driveway, then they sped to the neighborhood entrance, earning a glare from Mr. Peabody as he shuffled to his mailbox. Once her absence became known, would he tell her friends he'd seen her leave in a hurry?

She felt a pang of remorse. Lisa, Barbara and several other neighbors had befriended her during her lonely, fright-filled pregnancy. Lisa had been by her side during Lily's birth. They had brought her meals and watched over Lily so Tessa could catch up on sleep. The women had been her support network, yet they hadn't known her entire identity was a lie. Now they would be left with questions that probably wouldn't be answered.

Tessa was barely able to keep from blasting through

every red light between them and the interstate exit. With only three intersections to go, she noticed a dark Cadillac Escalade easing out of the library parking lot on their right. A second, identical one trailed the first.

Her fingers dug into the wheel. The bright April sun glinted off their windshields, searing her eyes. The light turned green, and she gunned it. The SUVs followed at a distance. As she drove through the last intersection and entered the long, deserted stretch between the town proper and the interstate, they sped up.

The one directly behind her bore down on her sedan and tapped her bumper.

Lily's chatter stopped. "Mommy?"

"It's all right, ladybug."

She put more pressure on the gas pedal. The car may have looked rickety, but thanks to Joey's expertise over at the local garage, the engine was in good shape. Thick stands of lofty pines formed natural walls on either side of the two-lane road. If she lost control, her car would be no match for them.

Please, Lord, I need Your help.

She'd become a believer soon after fleeing New Jersey. Her personal relationship with Christ meant everything to her. He was her protector, her best friend, her counselor. She trusted the Scriptures and, in them, He promised to never leave or forsake her.

The SUV struck her car again, with more force this time. The wheel jerked. The back end lurched, pointing her hood toward the road's edge and the grass between asphalt and unyielding trees. Her palms were slippery, and she had trouble righting the vehicle. Lily began crying in earnest.

Up ahead, a semitruck loaded with logs was chugging onto the road. If she could make it in time, he would block the SUVs.

Sending up another fervent prayer, she stomped on the gas pedal. The trees outside became a blur. The trucker saw her and blasted his horn. The logo plastered on the driver's door got larger and larger. Sweat dripped beneath her collar, and she couldn't catch her breath.

At the last second, she swerved. Entered the oncoming lane. A red sports car stared her down. Honked and flashed their lights. She wasn't going to make it. Mason's face flashed in her mind. He would never meet his daughter.

Tessa pushed the old car to go faster. "Please, please, please—"

Finally, she cleared the semitruck and jerked back into the right lane with seconds to spare. The sports car was a blur as he zipped by in the opposite direction. The rearview mirror gave her the news she'd prayed for. The SUVs were stuck behind the truck. She had mere minutes to disappear.

Tessa zoomed past the interstate exit. Dante would expect her to take it. Several miles past the exit, she turned into a truck stop and parked behind the building. Sweaty, shaky and not entirely sure they were safe, she twisted in her seat and worked on calming Lily. Long minutes passed before the little girl's sobs quieted. A juice box and pack of fish-shaped crackers helped restore calm.

"I don't like this 'venture," she mumbled, stuffing crackers into her mouth.

"We're going to the mountains," she told her in the brightest voice she could muster. "To Tennessee. It's beautiful there. You're going to love it."

"Do they have story time?"

She smiled. "I'm positive."

That wasn't all. Serenity, Tennessee, was where she'd met and fallen in love with a police officer. Those months with Mason Reed had been blissful, a brief span of stability and normalcy far from the reaches of her Mafia family. Until he'd left her with no explanation, of course, breaking her heart in the process.

Would he reject her again? Or would he agree to protect her and their daughter?

Mounted Police Sergeant Mason Reed sat astride his equine partner, Scout, and surveyed the scores of people who'd turned out for the annual spring event. He used to like the hot-air-balloon festival. Now, it was a raw reminder of his gullibility.

Beside him, Foster "Silver" Williams hefted a disagreeable sigh. "I know that look."

Mason didn't bother sparing him a glance. "You must have a smudge on your sunglasses."

"No smudge. This is the look you get every year around this time. Don't think I don't recall the significance."

Silver, nicknamed such because his hair had gone gray prematurely, had been with Mason the day his world had disintegrated. He and Tessa were supposed to have met up at the hot-air-balloon festival. Her brother had shown up instead.

"It's been almost four years. Time to let it go." Shifting in his saddle, Silver waved his gloved hand across the horizon like a wand. "Women can't resist the uniform or the horse. You should use them to your advantage."

Silver's cream-colored gelding, Lightning, swished his tail and bobbed his head, as if in agreement. A reluctant smile curved Mason's mouth. "There's a woman out there who will make you regret that cavalier attitude one of these days."

"I'm not a commitment kind of guy," he said, shrugging. "And I don't pretend otherwise. You, my friend, pine for home and hearth, and there's no reason why you can't have it. You were with her how long?"

He inhaled deeply. "Eleven months." And five days, to be exact.

"Eleven months is not enough time for her to qualify as the love of your life. I say put the past behind you, once and for all, and start searching for your forever girl."

Mason had dated off and on. Nothing had stuck. Some had complained he was emotionally closed off. He had Tessa to thank for that. Because of her betrayal, he hadn't been able to trust anyone new.

His radio chirped, and Serenity's other two mounted police officers, Raven Hart and Cruz Castillo, checked in.

"How's things at your end?" Mason asked.

"Uneventful," Raven said, her voice crackling over the radio.

"That's what I like to hear. We'll head your way in a few."

Raven and Cruz had chosen to patrol the fields where the balloons were tethered until their release at sunset. The blue-green mountains rose to sloping, gentle peaks in the distance, offset by a jewel-blue sky. Mason and Silver were covering the more densely populated area around Glory Pond, where paying customers could ride paddleboards and canoes. At the far end, Black Bear Café offered indoor and outdoor seating. A temporary stage had been set up beside the expansive brick patio, and plucky bluegrass tunes intertwined with laughter and crying babies. A bicycle-and-boat-rental shop was situated in the shelter of old-growth trees. Picnic tables were interspersed in the welcome shade. Beyond the trees, food trucks were parked in the cement lot between the pond and town square, offering everything from gourmet grilled-cheese sandwiches to mochi ice cream.

He and Silver had stationed themselves beneath the tallest trees for a temporary reprieve from the heat.

A towheaded girl of about ten approached. "Excuse me, sir, may I pet your horse?"

Mason leaned forward and slid his hand along Scout's neck. "Scout would be offended if you didn't."

She giggled and gingerly touched his nose. "How old is he?"

"Six. A farm up in Gatlinburg donated him to our unit. He's a Tennessee Walker."

She admired his chestnut body and flaxen hair. Scout had an easygoing disposition, and he lapped up the affection. Not far away, a couple waited and watched with fond smiles. The loneliness inside Mason throbbed like a dull headache that never quite went away. He angled his face so that Silver wouldn't notice and comment. His partner and friend, for all his swagger and smooth talk, was surprisingly intuitive.

Silver handed her a pair of small business cards. "Each horse on the mounted patrol unit has one," he explained. "Their picture is on the front, and their bio is on the back."

"Neat. Thank you."

"You're welcome."

Her parents beckoned her, and she skipped away. He watched the trio weave through the crowd and stop at a lemonade vendor.

Mason sensed Silver's keen gaze on him.

"That's it," he declared. "I'm creating an online dating profile for you."

"You wouldn't dare."

"Why not? You're obviously not going to look for love on your own…" He sat straighter in the saddle, the hollows in his cheeks more pronounced.

Mason looked around for signs of trouble. "What?"

"It can't be—" Silver snapped his mouth shut. His gloves creaked and strained over his bunched hands. Lightning nickered.

Mason didn't see anyone who'd indulged in too much alcohol. No physical altercations brewing. Serenity was tucked into the mountains of East Tennessee and was one of several gateway towns to Great Smoky Mountains National Park. Because of that, their population swelled April through October, bringing unique challenges to local law enforcement. Millions of visitors traveled through their town each year. Some drove through, stopping for a meal or to fuel up, while others took advantage of the various campgrounds, cabin rentals and motels. Not all were law-abiding citizens.

At the moment, he didn't recognize any laws being broken. "I can't read your mind, you know."

Muttering under his breath, Silver pointed to the cluster of blue canopies offering a range of kids' activities. The nearest one was face-painting central. His gaze probed the occupants, eventually landing on a woman standing apart from the group. Average height and weight. Casual but neat attire. She was a woman whose appearance—black hair, olive skin and striking features—would draw second and even third glances.

He'd recognize her anywhere. Her hair was thicker and fuller, the glossy curls sliding over her shoulders as she searched for someone or something. Sunglasses covered her eyes, but he knew the curve of her cheek, the straight line of her nose, the generous mouth almost always primed with shell pink gloss.

He almost fell off his horse.

What was Tessa doing here?

She bent and hefted a little girl into her arms, a girl with matching ringlets and dark eyes.

His skin stretched too tightly over his cheekbones. His teeth ground together. Denial spiraled inside, pulsating white-hot through his veins. Tessa was married. She had a child. She'd moved on. Suddenly, he was furious at himself for letting her steal four years of his life.

"I can handle this," Silver drawled. "I'd be happy to, in fact."

He would never admit it aloud, but he considered the offer. He didn't want to hear about Tessa's wonderful life, her devoted husband and child.

The decision was taken out of his hands the moment he noticed men closing in on her. A pair of muscle-bound men in black clothing, telltale bulges at their hips hinting at firearms. Tessa noticed and tensed, gathering her daughter closer to her.

"They're not here to see the balloons, I gather," Silver commented.

When one made a grab for the little girl, Mason urged Scout into action.

"Out of the way!"

He alerted the people blocking his path of his intent, and they quickly accommodated him and Scout. He had to repeat the command multiple times. The last thing he wanted was for an innocent bystander to be stepped on or knocked off balance.

Silver and Lightning were close behind. Over the radio, his partner alerted Raven and Cruz.

Tessa's scream unleashed a wave of alarm through the

crowd. The goons noticed the horses' rapid approach and took off. Silver thundered after them.

Mason hauled Scout to a halt and slid to the ground.

Tessa's shoulders eased when she saw him. There was no flash of recognition. When they'd dated, he'd been a patrol officer. She wouldn't know he'd accepted a position with the mounted-police unit.

"It's okay, Lily." Silent tears streamed down the child's cheeks, and her tiny shoulders shook with sobs. "You're safe. The police officer is here. He'll help us."

He took Scout's lead with one hand and her elbow with the other. "Come with me, Tessa."

His voice, and that he knew her name, must've registered, because she whipped up her head to focus fully on him. Her lips parted. Her eyebrows descended behind her glasses. "Mason?"

"This way."

Using his body as a shield, he hustled them through the curious onlookers, past the pond and to the Serenity mounted-police tent. He secured Scout to an oak tree and led Tessa inside. It was spacious enough to accommodate twenty-five people or more, and the white canvas provided much-needed privacy. A couple of tables had been set up to hold snacks and drinks. He slid out a folding chair and pointed. She complied without a word.

He removed his glasses and helmet, threading his fingers through his damp, rumpled hair. She watched him, her body taut and coiled, her arm curved protectively around the girl.

"Why are you here, Tessa?"

Her pallor became more pronounced. She, too, removed her glasses. Her hazel gaze slammed into him.

"I came to find you."

TWO

Suspicion chased disbelief across his rigid features. Surely the anger swirling in his brown eyes wasn't directed at her? He was supposed to have greeted her with an apology, or at least a blush of shame for what he'd done to her. Tessa was light-headed from the high emotions battling for supremacy.

He had grown more handsome with time. Slightly over six feet, he was sleek power in a deceptively trim frame. He had bronze skin, molten eyes the color of a rabbit's pelt and rich, thick brown hair.

After too many long, lonely years, mere inches separated her from the man who'd ripped the sun from her sky. She was supposed to despise him. She hadn't ever learned to do what she was supposed to, though. If she had, she would've done her father's bidding and married one of his Mafia associates. She'd have been like her mother, bearing children into a legacy of violence.

His upper lip curled. "What could you possibly want with me?"

This wasn't the thoughtful, kind man who'd wooed her with home-cooked meals, horseback rides and random gifts of chocolate. This wasn't the man who'd plagued her dreams, the man she'd wept buckets of tears over.

Her Mason wasn't capable of such an ugly expression. With that intense darkness enveloping him, he could have blended right into her Mafia family.

A shudder rippled through her. "My brother wants me dead. I caught him conspiring to kill a police officer and tried to prevent it."

Tessa licked her dry lips, wishing she could unsee the photos Dante had shoved in her face. Despite her best efforts, she hadn't been able to save Officer Fisk.

Mason folded his arms over his chest, an action that pulled the crisp, blue-black uniform tight across his shoulders. "How many brothers do you have? Because the one I met didn't strike me as a cold-blooded killer."

Dizziness washed over her. "You met Dante? When?"

He gave a minuscule shrug. "Doesn't matter. Go on."

"I approached Officer Fisk. He asked if I'd be willing to record evidence of their plans."

"Their?"

"My father and Dante. There are things you don't know about me, Mason."

He stared at her for long moments, then his gaze slid to Lily. "Clearly."

The possibility that Lily could be his daughter obviously hadn't entered his mind. He must think she was married or divorced. Tessa began to question her decision to come to him. He'd left her without a word, not even a text message or email. Why would he care that she was in danger? She wasn't even convinced he'd protect Lily. Sure, he'd mentioned having children someday. But it was clear he hadn't wanted any with her.

She stood up so quickly spots danced before her eyes. "This was a mistake."

His hand was gentle on her shoulder, steadying. "Hold on. Let me get you a drink."

Mason strode to the tables and made his choices. He brought back a bottle of water and orange juice. "Does she like this kind?"

Sinking to her seat, she took the juice from him. "Would you like some, Lily?"

Her daughter had plastered her cheek in the curve of Tessa's neck. Now, she lifted her head and reached out, peering shyly at Mason from beneath her curls.

"I like horses," Lily blurted.

He acted surprised she was talking to him. "You do?"

"Mommy bought me lots of horse books. Tillie's pink. Her sister's name is Toni, and she's purple."

His wide gaze assessed Lily, and Tessa wished she could read his thoughts. Did he see anything of the Reed family in her? Most people said she resembled Tessa, but there were certain gestures that reminded her of Mason.

"My horse's name is Scout," he said. "He helps me do my job."

Lily sat up. "Can I ride him?"

"That depends. Scout's particular about who rides him, but I'll tell you a secret." Lowering his voice, he said, "His favorite snack is peppermints."

Lily clapped her hands together. "I like peppermints, too."

His lips curved into a semblance of a smile. Tessa's heart flip-flopped.

There was movement at the tent entrance, and Mason's hand instinctively reached for the gun at his waist. Another officer entered, and Mason relaxed. "Well?"

"They jumped into a waiting SUV. We lost them. The sheriff's department will be on the lookout."

He removed his helmet. Sweat dampened his gray hair. The color should've been odd on a man in his late twenties, but combined with his fair complexion, angular features and vivid violet eyes, it gave him a unique look.

She'd met Mason's friend several times and liked him, despite his seize-the-moment, live-for-today approach to life.

"Hello, Tessa." His smile was more feral than charming. "What brings you to Tennessee?"

His tone conveyed he wished that she'd stayed away. She dismissed the objection forming on her lips. She wasn't here for answers or apologies. Lily's future was at stake.

"Lily, would you like to watch a video on my phone?"

She nodded and accepted the juice bottle. After settling her at the table in the corner, Tessa rejoined the men in the middle of the tent.

"I'm in trouble. My last name isn't Elliott. It's Vitale. You may have heard of my father, Antonio. His nickname is Bloody Tony."

Silver grunted and pinched the bridge of his nose. "Who hasn't heard of him?"

Mason's hands slipped from his hips. "You didn't think it was necessary to tell me this before? Did they know you were dating a cop?"

"No! Not until the very end. I wouldn't have put you in danger, not for anything in the world." His eyes darkened, and his jaw twitched. "I didn't know what my family was until I was thirteen. I would've run away then if I could have. When it was time for college, I convinced my father to let me come to Tennessee. I adopted the surname Elliott and didn't share many details of my past. I was supposed to go home every summer, but after the first one, I made sure I had an internship to keep me in Knoxville. I defied my father again after graduation when I got an apartment and job here. He and Dante had decided I should marry the son of another powerful family. The marriage would've cemented our families' alliance." She grimaced. "Dante would've come immediately to fetch me, but he was tied up with pressing business. That's why you and I had almost a year together."

He passed a weary hand over his face.

Silver paced closer. "Is Dante's goal the same as it was back then?"

"Dante wants me dead. He will take her to New Jersey once he's dealt with me."

Mason's watchful gaze fell on Lily. "How long have you been on the run?"

"Since the early days of my pregnancy." He actually winced. "At the police's request, I agreed to wear a listening device and try to gain a confession. My father's health was ailing, and he's always had a soft spot for me. I thought I could get him to talk about the plans for Officer Fisk, something that would hold up in court. Dante was tipped off by my sister, Francesca, and burst into the room. He would've killed me right then and there if Father hadn't intervened. I was locked in my bedroom for days. Dante showed me the photographs of Fisk's body, and he promised to do the same to me. By that time, I knew I was expecting. I had to escape. I wound up in small-town Georgia, and that's where we've been until yesterday."

Tessa could see the puzzle pieces start to fit together, could see him go ghostly pale beneath his tan. His eyes flashed to hers, as sharp as a rapier.

"How old is she, Tessa?"

"She turned three last month."

Silver bowed his head, squeezed his friend's shoulder and left the tent. The air became stifling, the cheery cartoon voices of Lily's video at odds with the anger and shock rippling through Mason.

"Is she mine?" he growled. "Or the other guy's?"

"What other guy?" she whispered, her brow puckering. "You were the only one."

Mason felt as if he might rip apart. Tessa may have been unfaithful, but she wouldn't keep his child from him.

"Look, I know the truth. Dante came to me and explained everything. He showed me the photos of you and your part-time boyfriend." His police-issue boots were uncomfortably tight, the bulletproof vest digging into his ribs. "Or was I the part-time one?"

"That's why you left without a word?" Her fingers dug into the spot over her heart, leaving imprints in her hunter green shirt. "Dante showed up at my apartment and demanded I go with him. When he saw a photograph of us on my mantel, he started asking questions. He was livid when he found out you were a cop. He threatened to hurt you, Mason. I tried to buy some time so I could tell you everything. Before I could, you'd left town."

"You were kissing another man in that photo."

"Are you sure it was me?" she challenged. "Give me your phone."

"What?"

"Take out your phone and search Francesca Vitale."

Mason did as she said and stared at the brunette on his screen. "Your sister?"

"She and I were close as children. Not anymore. She ratted me out when I was trying to help Fisk. You don't think she could've curled her hair and kissed someone just to serve Dante's purposes? He wanted me home, and he employs unusual methods to get what he wants."

And now, according to her, he wanted her dead.

He thrust his fingers through his hair and closed his eyes. He hadn't seen the woman's face, only a side view. Francesca looked enough like Tessa that it would've been easy to mistake the two. Since Tessa hadn't told him the truth about her family, he'd had no reason to doubt Dante's account.

But you're a police officer. Aren't you supposed to sniff out the bad guys?

"You didn't cheat?"

"No," she choked out.

He closed his eyes and prayed he wouldn't embarrass himself and fall to the ground in a dead faint. Slowly, he opened his eyes and looked at the little girl perched on the folding chair. His *daughter*.

"Did you know? When you left?" he murmured, his voice sounding like sandpaper.

"It wasn't until I was in New Jersey. When I finally figured it out, I tried to think how I could tell you. Keep in mind, I had no idea why you left or why you refused to talk to me."

"That's no excuse," he countered, swiping the air with his hand. "I missed her birth, her first words, steps, everything."

"I'm sorry, Mason." Her eyes begged him to understand. "Try and consider it from my point of view. My father, Antonio, and Dante don't think twice about killing someone they view as a threat to their plans. You were better off not being involved. Safer."

"Then why come to me now?"

"Because, if Dante succeeds in killing me, you can take her somewhere safe and raise her to be a decent human being."

THREE

Tessa was a bundle of nerves as Mason navigated the congested streets. Her most treasured memories of Tennessee were rooted in this town. Nestled in a picturesque valley amid lush, forested mountains, Serenity was magazine-worthy. They passed the central, parklike square framed with shops, cafés and the early twentieth-century courthouse.

Pangs of nostalgia were swallowed whole by Dante's vendetta. Was he watching them even now?

Silver had retrieved their belongings and Lily's car seat from Tessa's vehicle. The Serenity PD was working in conjunction with the sheriff's department in the search for her brother. Silver and the other mounted police officers would stay and manage the event while Mason got them to a safe place.

"Are you still living in the riverside duplex?" she asked.

"I bought a house last year."

Tessa glanced over, taking in his profile and marble-cast body. She could've bounced a nickel off his forearm—he was clenching the wheel with that much force. He wasn't happy with her. All this time, he'd believed she'd betrayed him. That he'd doubted her loyalty, that he'd accepted without question her flawed character, made her want to shake him. But part of the blame rested on her shoulders. He hadn't known her brother's true nature because she hadn't been forthcoming about her past.

Now he had another reason to despise her—keeping their child a secret.

Lily hummed a popular church hymn in the double cab's second row, clutching her ponies to her and staring at the passing scenery. Her lids were growing heavy.

"Does she do that a lot?" he asked quietly.

"Hum when she's sleepy? Yeah."

He sighed. "My mom has said I used to do that when I was little."

"Oh."

The hurt in his voice brought tears to her eyes. Sliding lower in the seat, she stared out the passenger window. She couldn't wish away his hurt, couldn't undo her decisions.

They left the town center behind and headed deeper into the foothills that marched alongside mountains and acres upon acres of protected forests. His spicy scent filled the truck cab. The traces of horse and leather were new, but not unpleasant.

A couple of miles later, he flicked the turn signal and guided the truck onto a ribbon of pavement. His driveway was a straight shot through the woods. The trees thinned to a clearing, revealing a white farmhouse with a red metal roof, shutters and front door. A wraparound porch invited visitors to enjoy a respite from the hot days. White and yellow rhododendron bushes brushed against the large windows. A flagstone path led around the house to a storage shed. It could've been a calendar photo for the month of April.

Once out of the truck, she studied the large willow tree trailing wispy fingers over the shed and a bubbling creek meandering to the woods. From here, she could see the top tip of a blue-green mountain.

"It's beautiful."

"It suits me." He avoided her gaze, gesturing to the house with his keys. "There are some things that still need attention, but everything works."

Tessa lifted Lily out of her car seat and, shifting her slumbering weight, climbed the porch steps. Mason went ahead of her and unlocked the door. She was glad she wasn't walking into a space rife with memories. Being near him was difficult enough.

Inside the foyer, she was met with ivory walls, shiny, mahogany floors and the bottom half of a staircase. To her left, sunlight drew colored diamonds across the planks and a cream throw rug. A round-armed denim couch faced the brick fireplace. A cloth ottoman stood in place of a coffee table, and the antique globe light fixtures could've been original to the home. On their right, shadows draped a formal study, allowing her a vague glimpse of a masculine desk, chair and built-in bookshelves.

Mason paused, looking uncertain. "She still takes naps?"

"Not every day. But we caught snatches of sleep in a roadside motel overnight. Yesterday and today's events have exhausted her."

"Do you want her on the couch? Or I have a guest bedroom upstairs."

"The bedroom will work."

His dark gaze seemed to soak in Lily. "Will she mind if I carry her up?"

Tessa took a step toward him. Lily didn't stir as she transferred her to Mason's arms. The sight of her daughter's pink, plump cheek resting against his broad chest, with her curls spread over his uniform, made Tessa's heart swell. This reunion hadn't been planned, but it was right.

He carried her to the second-floor hallway and turned left. There were four rooms in all, two bedrooms on this end and another bedroom, possibly the master, shared the other end with a hall bath. He went inside the room that looked out over the rear of the property. A fluffy, powder blue rug was splashed over the refurbished floorboards and anchored with a white frame double bed. A white coverlet with dainty blue sprigs topped the mattress. Matching curtains hung at the windows. A single dresser was stationed against the outer wall and a mirror above it. The furnishings were sparse, but the home was welcoming.

Mason placed her on the bed and covered her with a quilt. He didn't immediately move away. He gazed down at her for multiple heartbeats, then he bent and brushed a kiss on her forehead. Feeling like an intruder, Tessa retreated to the hall.

Taking their relationship beyond the proper boundaries hadn't been part of God's plan. She hadn't realized it then. Now that she had a personal relationship with Christ, she basked in His forgiveness and the promise of new mercies each morning.

Downstairs, he led her through the living room to the kitchen, which ran the length of the house. A new fridge was out of place in the worn work area. The cabinet paint was peeling, and some of the doors hung at odd angles. The sink was stained with rust. At the far corner, a rough-hewn table and chairs sat in front of a window with a forest view.

"Coffee?"

"Yes, please."

He rummaged through the cabinets and removed a pair of mugs. Once he had the machine set to brew, he pointed to a room out of sight and around the corner from the table.

"I'm going to get out of this gear. Milk's in the fridge. Sugar is in that jar. Help yourself."

Tessa hesitated. In the past, she'd been completely at home among his belongings. They'd often cooked together in his cramped duplex kitchen. Actually, she'd done the prep work under his direction, and he'd done the cooking. Her mouth watered just thinking about his spaghetti Bolognese.

He returned wearing a black Serenity mounted police cotton shirt, faded jeans and scuffed tennis shoes. A streamlined, black-and-white watch cradled his wrist. His hands were bare of other jewelry. With a start, she realized he could be in a serious relationship and that her sudden appearance might cause trouble.

She licked her dry lips. "Is anyone going to be bothered by my presence here?"

He arched a brow. "Besides me?"

The verbal shot wasn't his style. At her grimace, he lowered his gaze.

"It didn't occur to me that you might have a wife or fiancée. I was focused only on getting away from Dante."

"There's no one," he said flatly.

Tessa hated that his answer pleased her. This trip wasn't about reuniting their family. It was about surviving Dante's vengeance.

Mason poured them both coffee, fixing hers as she'd preferred before, half milk and two dashes of sugar. He walked the length of the kitchen and gestured to the table. She sat and cupped the mug between her hands. He stared out the window...formidable and untouchable.

"I know you have questions," she ventured. "I'll answer them to the best of my ability."

"Tell me about Lily."

"She's spunky. Sweet. She gets cranky when she's hungry."

He grunted. "Like you."

"I make sure to keep snacks with us," she said. "Her favorite food at the moment is grilled chicken. She likes any type of fruit. She dislikes green beans and refuses to try mashed potatoes or macaroni and cheese."

He finally turned his gaze on her. "I thought those were standard fare for kids."

"I thought so, too."

"How do you support yourself? Was she born on time? Were there any complications? She looks healthy. Is she?"

Tessa blinked, and he inhaled sharply. He pulled out the chair opposite and lowered himself into it. "I have a hundred questions. I don't even know where to start."

"Ask me whenever they come to you." She pressed her palms to the warm mug, hoping he didn't notice her nervousness. "The pregnancy was uneventful. I didn't gain as much weight as the doctor would've liked—"

"You didn't have enough money for food?" His eyes were so very dark, his eyelashes thick and inky black. She wished he'd look at her like he used to, when he'd thought she was interesting and beautiful and fun.

Those days are gone forever.

"It wasn't that. I just found it difficult to eat. My worry about being found didn't help the nausea any." Tessa had spent the first months reeling from Mason's abandonment and the fact she was, by all definitions, a fugitive. "Lily arrived a week before her due date, but she was perfect. No health concerns. Normal weight."

"I'm glad you were both okay," he said solemnly.

"When I left New Jersey, I took jewelry I'd received over the years and sold it piece by piece. It was enough to cover room rentals and food. Once I settled on Walton, I found a small home to rent for a decent price. And I started working when she was three months old. I got a job at our church's day-care program so that I could have her with me."

His eyebrows winged up. "You go to church?"

"This may surprise you, but my priorities have changed. My life is now centered around my faith in Jesus."

"I try to live the same way." His gaze roamed her face, regret twisting his features. "I wish I could say the same about when we were together." Before she could comment, he said, "What are her favorite things to do?"

"She loves to color and paint. Anything that's messy, really. She wants to learn how to bake cookies, and not the premade, tear-apart kind. I've promised to find someone to teach her when she gets older. I take her every week to the library's story hour." Her smile faded. "That's where we were yesterday when Mrs. Smith tipped me off."

"How do you think he tracked you down?"

"I don't know for sure." She hadn't accessed her old social-media accounts and had paid cash for literally everything.

"I wish you'd have come to me back then. We could've figured it out."

"I did what I thought was best for you," she said, knowing he would never understand. He hadn't lived her reality, hadn't seen what Dante was capable of. "And for our unborn child. If Dante found me here, he might've killed you out of spite."

His fingers balled. "Yet you risked untold dangers by heading into the unknown. I'm a cop, Tessa. I could've found a way to protect you."

"Cops are his favorite targets."

The words were automatic, a whisper of the past. Their truth had faded enough for her to choose this town, this man, as her safe haven. Too late, she remembered Fisk's terrible death. She pressed her hand to her mouth.

"I should've gone west, not east." Shoving out of her seat, she lurched to the window, leaned on the sill and drew in deep breaths.

He came up behind her. "What did you say?"

She pressed her forehead to the cold glass and closed her eyes. "I didn't stop to pray or consider. I heard his voice on the surveillance system, and I panicked. That's what he wanted. To keep me from making the right move."

"Tessa, coming here was the right move. If you hadn't, I would still be in the dark about my child."

"But at what price?"

Tessa's fear was palpable. Fear for *him*. Kind of difficult to swallow after all these years of thinking she'd played him for a fool.

He didn't know if he was angrier at her or himself. He hadn't been looking for a relationship that long-ago afternoon when he'd come upon Tessa's vehicle, her tire busted and no spare in the trunk. Her unruly curls and winsome smile had enchanted him. As he'd taken her in his cruiser to the nearest automotive-parts place, he'd become intrigued by her. She was passionate about her work pairing foster kids with loving couples. From that one conversation, he'd glimpsed her heart for service, and that mirrored his own life path. By the time they'd returned to her car and gotten the tire patched, he'd known she was someone special. His instincts had been right. She was not only kind and quick to defend the weak, but she also had a zest for life. He'd fallen for her, plain and simple.

Tessa was the only woman who'd inspired thoughts of wedding rings and lifelong commitment. Near the end, she'd gotten distracted and anxious, and he'd panicked. He'd made the mistake of thinking that taking the next step in their relationship would fix things.

When Mason had believed she'd been unfaithful, he couldn't see her or talk to her without damaging her with his words. He'd been that decimated.

He should've given her a chance to explain.

"It's too late to switch courses," he said. Her silken hair was a curtain around her face. He prayed she wouldn't break down, because he wasn't sure he'd be able to resist holding her. "Tell me what I need to know about your brother."

Her shoulders lifted and fell. "There's no mercy in him. No compassion." She faced him, her eyes telling tales of a sinister history. "He thrives on other people's misfortunes. Once he sets his mind to something, he won't be dissuaded."

"You said your father stopped him from killing you."

"Our father is the only person Dante will heed. His health is failing, however. I've kept up with Vitale news through local papers and social-media accounts. I don't know that he could stop this. I don't know where I stand with Father anymore, not after I acted against them."

Mason was having trouble understanding how such a family operated and how it could've produced Tessa.

"He's five years older than me," she continued. "Seven years separate him and Fran. He disdained spending time with us because, in his mind, he was more worldly and important. While Fran and I were playing with puppies in the garden, he was being molded into the Vitale second-in-command. It wasn't until I stumbled into one of their retaliation kills that he started paying attention to me."

She pressed her lips together and smoothed her hair behind her ears.

"It wasn't the kind of attention you wanted."

Her eyes awash in misery, she shook her head. Mason was tempted to cup her cheek and smooth his thumb across the soft, freckle-dusted skin. How could she have hidden this part of her life from him for so long?

He shoved his hands in his pockets. "How old were you?"

"Thirteen." She closed her eyes. "I came to the receiving room in search of Father. I'd won some certificate at school... I can't remember now what it was. Father and his men didn't see me, but Dante did. He shoved me behind the couch, covered my mouth and made me watch as they stabbed that man again and again. It wasn't a slow death," she whispered bleakly.

Mason blew out his breath and switched his attention to a bluebird perched on the feeder outside. He'd let a ruthless killer convince him that Tessa was the one without morals. He'd basically driven her back to that place of torment, and she'd been carrying his baby.

His eyelids pricked. Tessa had been vulnerable and alone.

Lord Jesus, thank You for keeping Your hand on them. Thank You for bringing Lily into my life. Please help me to be the kind of father You want me to be. Help me keep them safe.

There was much, much more he needed to know, but he couldn't digest any more at this moment. Before he could suggest she rest for a while, the window to their right exploded. Glass shattered. The distinct whistle of a bullet registered, followed by Tessa's scream.

Mason grabbed her. Shoved her beneath the table and slid into the space with her.

"You hurt?"

Her eyes were panic-stricken. "No. You?"

Another shot whizzed inside, digging into the Sheet-rock behind them. The shooter was on the move, getting closer.

"Stay here. I'm going outside."

"Mason, don't." She seized a fistful of his shirt.

He placed his cell in her hand. "Call Silver."

Then he snagged his pistol from the counter and went in search of the enemy.

FOUR

Mason crouched in the screened-in porch and searched for the glint of a rifle scope among the trees. The sun's angle was unfortunate, and the slanting rays made his unprotected eyes water. He shifted to ease a leg cramp, and a bullet pierced the screen near his head, pinged off the patio table and burrowed into the wood siding.

Above the drumming of his heart, he heard sirens echoing off the mountains. An engine revved out of sight. A blur of black caught his eye. Before he could take aim, a door slammed and tires burned against pavement.

He shoved through the porch door and rushed to the corner of the house, pressing close to the facade. Peering around the edge, he glimpsed the tail end of a Cadillac Escalade as it sped down his driveway.

Mason retraced his steps. Inside the kitchen, glass bits crunched beneath his sneakers. A honeysuckle-scented breeze seeped through the open fissures and stirred the curtains. The chairs around his table were disturbed and the space beneath was empty.

"Tessa?"

After looking in the utility room and first-floor bath, he strode the length of the house, checking other windows for damage. She wasn't in the living room or the office. The front door was secure. His pulse began to gather speed. Had they lured him out back on purpose? Had they gotten to her? To Lily?

He pivoted and was about to scale the stairs when her ballet flats tapped down the wooden treads. She'd had at least two dozen pairs when he'd known her, and these were black with a subtle sparkle. Next, her tailored black pants came into view, a silver band around her wrist and finally her scoop-neck shirt and slinky earrings. Her features creased with worry when she saw him.

"Are you okay? I was upstairs when I heard the second shot."

His grip on the pistol eased slightly. "I'm good. Lily?"

"Still asleep." Reaching the foyer, she held out his phone. "Silver promised to send help. Did you see Dante?"

"There was one shooter in the woods. He heard the sirens the same time I did. I didn't get a good look at him, but I saw a single SUV."

Moving into the living room, he stationed himself at the edge of the picture window and monitored the yard while he contacted police dispatch. One of the mounted-police-unit trucks pulled through the trees and parked behind his. A low-slung black Corvette jerked to a stop farther down the drive.

Tessa had come to stand beside him, close enough that her particular scent, a blend of vanilla and cinnamon, taunted him.

"I need to brief my unit."

Nodding, she turned her attention on the officers exiting the truck. Mason tucked his Glock in his rear waistband, about to trade the cool interior for the balmy evening. He descended the porch steps, meeting Cruz and Raven halfway. They were still in uniform but had left their helmets in the truck.

Silver's car alarm chirped, and he pocketed his keys as his long strides ate up the tender green grass.

"What's going on?" Cruz looked from Mason to the house. The newest member of the unit, he had transferred from Texas last year. He'd shared snippets of his previous life, although not enough to gain a clear picture.

"Full disclosure. The woman inside the house is Tessa Vitale, daughter of Antonio Vitale. You may have heard of him."

Raven whistled. "Bloody Tony. What's she doing in our neck of the woods?"

The tips of Mason's ears burned. He didn't relish revealing his private business, but these three had his back, no matter what. "I knew her as Tessa Elliott. We were once in a serious relationship, and she's returned requesting my protection. Apparently, Antonio is in poor health and is slowly relinquishing his duties to his heir, Dante." He explained her involvement with the unfortunate Officer Fisk. Their expressions darkened with dismay. "The little girl with her, Lily, is my daughter." Saying it out loud for the first time choked him up. Staring at his boots, he used the ensuing silence to mentally regroup. "I understand you're as shocked as I am."

"She didn't tell you?" Raven demanded, outraged on his behalf.

He lifted his gaze. "Tessa and I have a lot to work through. I know I can count on you to treat her with respect."

Cruz inclined his head, a silent show of support. Raven clamped her lips together. Silver's gaze was probing, solemn. Then his famous grin flashed, and he looped his arm around Mason's shoulders. "This makes me an honorary uncle, right? I'm going to spoil her rotten."

Mason actually smiled. Inside the house, he left the others in the living room and followed the sound of tinkling glass. Tessa was sweeping up the broken bits and didn't look up at his approach.

"I'll take care of that later." His voice was gruffer than he'd intended. Her presence in his home was throwing him off-kilter.

She propped the broom against the wall. When she came near, he said, "I told the others about our connection and about Lily."

"I figured." A flush worked its way up the slender column of her neck.

"They have to know the facts if they're going to help."

"I understand, Mason."

Tessa remained at the room's edge, using the armchair as a shield. Cruz and Raven sat on opposite ends of the sofa, and Silver leaned against the fireplace, arms crossed. Awkward tension hung in the room. Silver offered a quiet greeting. The other officers merely nodded in reaction to his introductions. Mason retrieved his laptop from his office and brought up Dante's image. Sour resentment rushed to the surface. This man had orchestrated his and Tessa's breakup. If not for him, Mason might've had a chance to attend his daughter's birth, to be involved in her early years.

Wrangling his focus on the matter at hand, he set the laptop on the ottoman and jerked a finger at the image. He hadn't changed much in the intervening years. Whipcord-lean and well over six feet, Dante carried himself like a prince and dressed like one, too.

"This is Dante Vitale. Thirty-one years old. Has a distinguishing scar above his left eyebrow. He's unmarried?"

"That's right," Tessa confirmed. "He's had an on-again, off-again relationship with a woman named Shelly Miles."

"New Jersey is home base. How many guards does he usually travel with?"

"Four. Bruno Esposito is the one who sticks like glue to my brother. He's a Mack truck." When Mason searched more images and angled the screen toward Tessa, she nodded. "Bruno's the grizzled one. Don't let his age fool you. He's in better shape than I am. And he's been in the Vitale service for decades. He won't hesitate to sacrifice himself for my brother."

"Do you recognize anyone else?" Cruz asked her.

Tessa leaned forward, resting her hands on the chair's curved top, and studied the screen again. "The short guy on the end, the one with the mustache, is James Lisowski. He's a follower, not an original thinker. I don't know the others."

"The license plate I glimpsed was from Georgia," Mason said. "I'm guessing Dante likes to travel in style."

"My father owns a private plane. They probably flew down and then rented vehicles."

Raven flipped her long black braid behind her shoulder. "They'll dump the Cadillacs. The tags make them easy to spot."

"Or they'll switch out the plates for locals and remove the rental stickers," Cruz said, rubbing his jaw.

Mason caught Silver's gaze. "What are you thinking?"

Uncrossing his arms, he pushed off from the mantel. "This guy's got wads of cash at his disposal. He can get his hands on weapons, getaway vehicles, you name it. He can pay for information or dirty jobs. That makes him more dangerous than most." His violet gaze fell on Tessa. "You're going to require twenty-four-hour protection."

Although what he said hadn't been an accusation, Tessa flinched.

"Let me be clear about something," Mason said, making eye contact with each of them. "I'm not asking any of you to go above and beyond the usual job requirements. We have our patrols and other cases. I don't expect anyone to put in extra hours on this."

Silver rolled his eyes. "Don't be so dramatic, brother. We're in this with you, one hundred percent."

Raven jutted her chin. "I'm willing to do whatever needs to be done."

Cruz left the couch to clap Mason's shoulder. "There's no doubt in my mind that you'd stick your neck out for us. I'd do no less for you, Sergeant."

"Thank you," Mason said gruffly, catching Tessa's touched expression.

"I'd like to thank you, too," she said. "I appreciate your willingness to help."

Raven and Cruz were all business, acknowledging her with solemn nods.

Raven swung her head, her long braid sliding along her crisp uniform. "Let's go, Cruz. We've got to see to the horses."

"I'll take guard duty tonight," Cruz offered.

"Already called it," Silver announced, smirking.

Cruz planted his hands on his utility belt, a teasing challenge in his eyes. "I didn't hear you call it."

"Then you weren't paying attention."

A disgruntled noise escaped Raven. She hooked her arm through Cruz's and tugged him toward the door. "When will you two stop acting like teenagers?"

Mason observed Tessa watching the interplay between his teammates. She must be aware of their loyalty to him and that they weren't thrilled with her. But she wasn't in a position to care whether they liked her or not. She was desperate for help, and that desperation had driven her to him.

He wished she'd come for different reasons, like his right to know he was a father. Despite the circumstances she'd found herself in, he couldn't completely let her off the hook. He wasn't sure he'd be able to forgive her, and that was a problem. Because they were going to have to work together to keep their daughter safe.

Yesterday morning, Tessa wouldn't have dreamed she'd be sharing a meal with Mason. As the years had passed, she'd thought of him often, reliving their many happy moments together. What she hadn't allowed herself to do was envision a reunion. It was too fraught with regrets and disappointments. Now, she was seated in his living room, and the reality was much worse than she'd feared.

He was painstakingly polite to her. When he did look at her, his face was a calm sea, while his eyes were twin hurricanes. They whipped at her, threatening to topple her. *How could you do this to me?*

Her reasons for staying away had seemed so right and solid when hundreds of miles separated them. Face-to-face, her logic disintegrated like a sand dune in gale-force winds. She hadn't calculated the depth of his hurt. She'd wounded *Mason*, the one person she never would've chosen to hurt, not in a million lifetimes.

The salted fry turned to dust in her mouth. Gulping orange soda—apparently Silver's idea of a proper drink for adults and toddlers alike—she begged God to stall her tears until she was alone.

I'm drowning here, Lord. Drowning. What have I done?

"I ordered chicken tenders, too, in case she didn't like burgers," Silver said, gesturing to Lily's plate.

Lily had taken off the bun and torn the patty into pieces. She hadn't eaten much. She'd awoken crying from her nap. The unfamiliar surroundings had scared her. Coming downstairs to find a roomful of uniformed officers hadn't helped. Cruz and Raven had quickly made themselves scarce, and Silver had contacted a meal-delivery service.

Mason had retreated to the kitchen, rid the floor of glass and nailed plywood over the broken window. For safety reasons, he'd set up a portable table in the living room, tucked between the wall and the couch. They'd be able to see anyone coming up the drive.

"Lily, would you like some chicken?" Tessa asked.

She shook her head and scooted her chair even closer to Tessa's. Lily hadn't spent much time around men, especially men in uniforms with badges and guns.

"I ordered pie for dessert. Does she like pie? It's pecan," Silver said. "Does she have any allergies?"

Mason had spoken very little during the meal, aside from saying a brief prayer of blessing. He was seated on her left, at the head of the table.

"Fortunately, no." Tessa looked across the table at Silver. "You've thought of everything. Thank you."

"You're welcome." His unusually colored eyes seemed to take her measure.

Tessa was glad for Silver's company, despite his reservations. He kept the meal from being conducted in complete, miserable silence. She noticed his habit of wearing long sleeves and leather gloves year-round hadn't changed. Her curiosity stirred. When she'd asked Mason the reason, he'd gotten a funny look and declined to answer.

"When are we going home, Mommy?"

Silver's hand stopped halfway to his mouth, the burger dripping juice onto his plate, and he snuck a furtive glance at Mason. Tessa didn't look at him. She couldn't.

"I'm not sure yet." She hadn't yet considered what exactly to tell Lily or how to explain their current circumstances.

Mason cleared his throat. "You don't want to leave before you see the stables, do you? We have six horses. You can help me feed them."

Lily's expression brightened. "Tonight?"

"My friends, Cruz and Raven, are already getting them tucked in. I thought we could go in the morning and feed them breakfast."

"Can I give them mints?"

Mason smiled. "They'd like that."

"What are their names? Are they boys or girls?"

Lily listened as he explained about the horses in their care. Tessa used the distraction to hand her daughter bits of meat and fries, which she ate without complaint. When they were finished, Silver retreated to the study to make phone calls.

Tessa cleared the wrappers and napkins, while Mason put leftovers in the fridge. Lily trailed behind him.

"Will you color with me?"

His brown eyes reflected surprised pleasure. "Do you like to draw? We could use blank paper and pens."

"There are crayons and coloring books in Lily's travel bag," Tessa suggested.

"I'll get them from the truck."

"Yay!" Lily bounced on her toes.

As soon as Mason brought in the bags, Lily dug in hers and removed almost all of the items until she found the crayons and books. Toddler-sized clothes and socks, along with baby dolls and toys, were now strewn across his

floor. Tessa recalled he liked to keep things tidy, but he
hadn't been obsessive about it. He patiently encouraged
Lily to replace her unwanted things, helping her along
the way. When the pair moved to the table and began
coloring together, Tessa felt out of place. Unneeded. In
Mason's mind, unwanted.

You don't have the right to feel sorry for yourself. Besides, he deserved Lily's undivided attention.

Tessa carried the bags upstairs and, for lack of anything better to do, transferred their belongings to the
dresser drawers. There was no way of knowing how long
they'd be staying, but she didn't think he'd mind. When
she finished, she waited in the open doorway, letting their
mingled voices waft up the stairs and over her.

*Lord Jesus, please protect us and lead law enforce-
ment to Dante. Please give Mason a chance to form a
lasting bond with Lily.*

She thought about asking God to not let Mason hate
her, but it seemed selfish.

Retrieving her Bible from the top drawer, she spent
the next half hour reading through her favorite Psalms.
She heard the study door open and close, and Silver's
voice as he addressed Mason. The front door creaked
and boots thudded on the porch.

Mason and Lily came looking for her not long after.

"Mason's a good colorer, Mommy," Lily said as she
scampered onto the bed.

"Is that so?" Tessa closed the heavy book and placed
it on the nightstand.

"Guess what? He used the glitter crayons."

Mason remained on the threshold, his hands in his
pockets. He looked as uncertain as she had felt earlier.
He took note of the Bible, and she could tell he was still
adjusting to the fact she was a believer. She could say

the same about him. As wonderful as their relationship had been, it hadn't been built on God's standards. Without Him as their foundation, they wouldn't have found lasting happiness together.

Tessa stood to her feet. "She usually takes a bath before bed. Do you mind?"

"Of course not." He twisted toward the hall. "There are fresh towels and washcloths in the linen closet."

"I didn't see Ducky in my bag," Lily announced.

"I'm afraid we left him at home."

"I can't take a bath without Ducky!"

Sensing the brewing meltdown, Tessa plucked her off the bed. "Ducky wouldn't want you to sleep in Mason's nice clean bed without washing off the dirt first. He'd be sad if you did."

She contemplated that. Mason slowly nodded. "Maybe we can find a friend for Ducky in one of the stores here."

"Can I take the new friend back home with me?"

His features shuttered. "That's a possibility."

Tessa felt like they were navigating emotional land mines. They couldn't make plans for the future until they'd dealt with the present.

Mason left them to their own devices. After Lily had bathed, brushed her teeth and climbed into bed, she asked if he could read her a bedtime story. Tessa found him downstairs on the couch, his laptop on his lap.

"Sorry to disturb you. Lily's requested that you read to her."

He closed the laptop. "Is that part of her bedtime routine?"

"It is."

"Books were a big part of your life."

"They always have been." They'd been her escape when life became difficult. "I've read to Lily since she was about six months old. Story time at the library is a long-standing tradition."

He looked at her, his gaze unreadable. "I'm glad you're passing that passion on to our daughter."

He gave her a wide berth and ascended the stairs. Tessa couldn't resist following him. He hadn't asked her to stay away, so she didn't.

"What are we reading?" Mason got comfortable on the bed, stacking pillows behind his back and stretching his legs out.

Lily's damp curls kissed her pink nightgown, and her cheeks were rosy from the warm bath. She snuggled close to him and handed him the book. "The horses are named Tillie and Toni."

"I remember you told me about them earlier today." He opened the book to the first page and began to read.

Tessa hovered in the hallway, thrilled with the sight of Mason and Lily together, like a father and daughter should be. She was also ensnared by the soothing cadence of his velvet-wrapped voice.

Lily must've found his voice just as soothing, because she fell asleep before the end. Mason gingerly got to his feet and, leaving the book on the nightstand, joined Tessa.

He pulled the door almost closed. "How did I do?"

"You're a natural."

"She keeps reminding me this isn't her home."

"Kids her age don't like change. Our departure was rushed and fraught with danger. Dante almost succeeded in running us off the road, and I had to skirt a log truck to put distance between us, in the process playing chicken with a sports car."

His face hardened. "You didn't tell me."

"I didn't have a chance to in the handful of hours we've been here."

He pinched the bridge of his nose. "I didn't mean to put you on the defensive."

"I'd say you're handling everything amazingly well."

"I want to tell her the truth about who I am."

"Okay."

"We'll tell her together, when the time is right. After the danger has passed."

"Dante won't be easily defeated or distracted from his goal."

"We'll be ready for him."

Tessa wanted to believe Mason, but he had no idea the depth of evil he was up against.

FIVE

Mason had been awake since two in the morning, when he and Silver had switched guard duty, but he was wired. It could be the gallon of coffee he'd downed. More likely, it was because his mind wouldn't rest. He had a daughter who was in serious danger of being abducted and an ex-girlfriend with a target on her back. His enemy had been groomed for crime since birth.

Muddling matters was the very real resentment clamoring for attention. Every time he thought about Lily's birth, her first birthday party, her first words—all the major milestones he'd missed—his heart spasmed with pain. Tessa had professed to love him. But if she really did, she wouldn't have robbed him of precious time with his daughter.

He *should* take his hurt to the Lord and ask for healing. Right now, he wanted to wallow in his anger, because forgiving Tessa meant what she'd done was okay. And it wasn't. Not by a long shot.

Mason drove past the courthouse. Tessa was hunkered against the passenger door, her focus on the lush green landscape that typified a wet spring in the Smokies. She had been withdrawn this morning, content to let Lily's chatter fill the silence. In the past, he would've pulled her

into a hug and rained kisses over her face until her trill-
ing laughter erupted. She must've sensed his attention,
because she shifted away from the window and looked
at him. She'd donned a fitted black jacket over a cotton-
candy-pink shirt and the same black pants and sparkly
flats from yesterday. Her lips were shiny with her favored
gloss. Silver cross earrings shimmered at her ears. The
striking combination of her dark, riotous hair and gold-
green eyes against her olive skin made him feel as if he'd
been kicked in the chest.

His fingers tightened on the wheel. She still affected
him. An annoying state of affairs, that.

"What day is it?" Lily asked.

"Sunday."

"I want to go to church."

Tessa sighed. "I wish we could, ladybug. Maybe next
Sunday."

Mason was glad Lily didn't press the issue. While
he would've liked to take her—and possibly Tessa, as
well—to his church, it wasn't safe. He usually attended
services after feeding and grooming the horses. This
morning, he'd be in a meeting with his immediate superior, Lieutenant Hatmaker. Hatmaker had called last night
and shared his extreme annoyance that Mason and Silver
had left the event prematurely. While he had a right to
his opinion, Mason was in charge of the horses and his
officers. He'd made the only decision open to him—get
Tessa and Lily to safety. Fortunately, the man in charge
of patrol division, Lieutenant Polk, would also be in the
meeting. He hoped they could review the case and agree
on a plan of action going forward.

"Here we are," he said, pointing to the unit stables.
They were located on the far side of town, beyond the
firehouse and police headquarters. While not as large

as the state's other units, the facility was more than adequate for both the horses and officers.

"I don't remember this being here," Tessa said.

"It's new, only open eighteen months. The old site was several miles outside of town and fairly run-down. We had several fundraising events to raise money. Private donors also pitched in."

The parking lot was enclosed by a tall, chain-link fence. Mason got out and unlocked the gate, then drove close to the building's side entrance. Silver had followed them from the house, and he took care of locking the gate.

"Why are the horses outside?" Lily strained to see the large paddock that ate up much of the property.

Mason liked her boundless curiosity and wonder over seemingly simple things. She was a bright, beautiful child. Of course, she took after her mother.

"They spend each night in the paddock, as long as the weather cooperates."

"Can I go inside there with them?"

"How about you and your mom watch as Silver and I lead them inside? Then you can help us feed and groom them."

She seemed satisfied with that as he released the restraints and hoisted her into his arms. Her weight was slight, her hair springy and soft, and she smelled like the syrup they'd doused their waffles in. He closed his eyes briefly to drink in the experience. When he opened them, he found Tessa watching him and Lily. He couldn't pin down one singular emotion in her wide eyes. He only knew that she was aware of what her choices had cost him.

Good. She *should* feel guilty and ashamed.

Will that really make you feel better?

Not comfortable with his thoughts or their exposed

position, Mason directed Tessa and Lily to stand just inside the stables' wide pass-through while he and Silver led the horses into the central area, a long, spacious aisle lined with stalls.

"It's time to groom the horses and give them a quick checkup." Mason positioned Scout in the middle of the aisle and attached ropes to his head collar. They waited as he gathered the grooming kit from the tack room.

Farther down the aisle, Silver was executing the same routine with Lightning.

Halfway through his routine, Mason noticed Lily was getting antsy. He started explaining the things he was checking on Scout.

"You check his teeth?" Her eyes got big. "Like a tooth doctor?"

"Like a dentist, exactly. A horse with a sore tooth can become very cranky." Beckoning Tessa closer, he said, "Have a look for yourself."

Adjusting Lily higher on her hip, Tessa approached and petted Scout's strong neck. "You do this every day?"

"Before we head out on patrol and after we return. If we find anything beyond our ability to treat, we call in the vet."

"I remember how much you enjoyed riding. Now that your job involves horses, do you find time to ride for fun?"

He and Tessa had been frequent customers of area riding stables. Their favorite was located in Cades Cove, inside the national park. "Not as often as I'd like." He snagged a dandy brush. "Do you want to brush him?"

"You don't mind?"

He held out his arms to Lily, who willingly came to him. He placed the brush in Tessa's palm and got out of her way. She was almost finished when Mason heard a feminine gasp coming from the side hallway, where the offices were located.

He turned and saw his sister staring at them with mouth agape.

Tessa slowly lowered the brush. "Candace."

Candace's eyes narrowed. "What brings you back to Serenity, Tessa?"

"I, ah—"

"Let's go to the break room, sis," Mason interrupted, lowering Lily to the ground.

Leaving Lily with Tessa, Mason took hold of Candace's arm and steered her the way she'd come. She resisted, and her head swiveled over her shoulder.

"Why aren't you at church?" Mason said, urging her forward.

Her blue gaze pierced him. "When my brother texts and asks if I have any spare toddler books at the day care and possibly a bath floaty, I get suspicious."

He flicked on the break-room light, ushered her inside and closed the door. She slapped a cloth bag on the nearest table and jammed her hands on her hips. "Why is she here, Mason? And why does that little girl have your eyes?"

"You think Lily has my eyes?"

She made a flustered sound. He might have inherited his mom's looks, but his sister had gotten her high spirits.

"Tessa sought me out because she needs protection from her brother." He explained her unfortunate family ties. "And, yes, Lily is my daughter."

"But she cheated on you."

"No, she didn't. That was a ruse to get me to leave her."

"She could be lying, you know."

"I believe her, Candace."

She thrust her hand through her pale hair, mussing the short strands. "She does look like you."

"The timeline is right."

"I can't believe you're a dad." She slapped her hand to her chest in typical dramatic style. "And I'm an aunt. Mom is going to flip! Have you told her?"

"I was planning on calling her sometime today." It wasn't a conversation he was looking forward to having.

"Promise me something," Candace urged. "Don't fall for her again. When you and Tessa were together, you were happy—insanely happy. I was jealous of what you guys had, in fact. But afterward…" She closed the distance between them and placed her hand on his shoulder. "Mason, I can't let you return to that bleak place."

He had no intention of letting that happen. "No need to worry. Tessa and I had our chance, and we blew it."

The rectangular office space wasn't meant for this many people. Officers in and out of uniform crowded around the boardroom-style table. Mason wielded a marker in front of a dry-erase board at the room's far end. Leadership was an easy mantle on his shoulders. He looked official in his Serenity PD T-shirt, which had a bear logo over his heart, cargo pants and military-style boots. His holstered weapon rested against his waist.

Tessa remained at the room's edge, seated apart from everyone, her chair straddling the open doorway. From this vantage point, she could see into the break room, where Candace was entertaining Lily. The petite blonde, opposite from Mason in looks and temperament, was clearly enamored with her niece. It made sense, since Candace loved kids. So much so that she'd opened her own day care.

Tessa and Candace had once gotten along like sisters.

Indeed, Tessa had thought that someday they'd be family. Candace had refused to take her calls following the breakup, and Tessa had eventually stopped trying. While she accepted that their friendship likely wasn't going to be restored at this point, she was thrilled for Lily. Her daughter would benefit from having a law-abiding family.

"Tessa?"

With a start, she realized everyone was staring at her. The mounted-police unit had been joined by Lieutenant Hatmaker, whose attitude suggested the milk in his coffee had soured, and men from the patrol division—Lieutenant Polk, Officer Bell and Officer Weiland.

Mason's eyebrows were raised. "We need more insight into Dante and how he operates," he said. "Does he dole out orders, or does he like to get his hands dirty?"

"A little of both, I guess. He lets his guards round up the target. If it's someone he wants to deal with personally, he has that person brought to a specified place." Her throat went dry. "He likes to toy with his victims."

Silver pushed his laptop to the center of the table. "The photos of Officer Fisk were leaked online. Is this Dante's handiwork?"

Tessa kept her gaze on her lap, her stomach churning. Those images were burned into her brain, and she had no desire to be subjected to them again. "Yes."

Ominous silence filled the space. She could feel their horror being directed at her. Her own sibling had committed atrocities against an officer. How could she be normal?

Cruz was the first to speak. "Where would he choose to stay when far from home base?"

She forced her gaze up. "A hotel is not ideal, with security cameras and witnesses. I'd say he would scout out a private residence and either pay for someone's silence or seize it."

"He'll find a place convenient to Mason's," Raven announced to the group. "I'll compile a list of nearby residences, focusing first on the rentals."

"Call my assistant Lindsey," Silver instructed. "She'll help you with the rentals I own."

"Will do."

Lieutenant Polk, a pleasant-faced gentleman, stated that he, Bell and Weiland would visit the homes in Mason's vicinity and warn residents to be vigilant. Other officers would contact local business owners.

When everyone began to file out of the room, Lieutenant Hatmaker squared off against Mason like an irate bulldog.

"This personal issue better not overshadow your other duties, Reed," he snapped. "If I see that it becomes a problem, I'll take my concerns to the chief."

Mason squared his shoulders. "My officers and horses are my top priority, as is protecting every member of this community. Dante Vitale is a threat to everyone in Serenity, not just Tessa. No one is safe with him running free."

Hatmaker's gaze flicked to Tessa, and he seemed to dismiss her out of hand. "Then we need to make sure he's caught soon."

He stalked into the hallway and joined Polk and the others. Mason closed the door behind him and rested against it.

"Is he always like that?" she asked.

"He has his days," he sighed. "We don't always see eye to eye. I have to do what's best for mounted patrol, and he's working on behalf of the department. Our goals sometimes clash, and we have to find ways to compromise."

Catching Dante was crucial for so many reasons. Tessa walked over to the board and reread the case notes. He came to stand beside her.

"I used to pretend I was adopted," she mused. "That I had a regular family somewhere."

"Did Dante ever hurt you?" His voice was like gravel.

The question threw her. She thought about her bruised and swollen throat after he'd strangled her, the slaps and pinches he'd doled out that their father knew nothing about.

"Tessa." Her name was a jagged whisper on his lips. His fingers closed over her hers, warm and comforting.

Tears sprung to her eyes. She hadn't expected compassion from him.

"It wasn't severe."

"Doesn't matter," he growled. "It's still abuse."

She merely nodded, the words on the board blurring.

"Did your mother know?"

"She lives in fear of both my father and Dante. She wouldn't have dreamed of intervening."

His fingers flexed on hers, then let go. "Did he torment your sister, too?"

Tessa finally met his turbulent gaze. "Growing up, Fran idolized Dante. That fed into his ego." She toyed with the jacket buttons on her sleeve cuffs. "My mother did help convince Father to let me attend an out-of-state university. I'm grateful for that."

"You said you chose UT Knoxville because a childhood friend vacationed in the Smokies."

"That's true. It only took one prospective college visit to convince me." She smiled, thinking about her freshman dorm room. "Some might think changing out a mansion for a cramped dorm would be a rough adjustment. That wasn't the case for me. I loved everything about campus life, mainly because it wasn't tainted by my Mafia roots. I went home that first summer because it was expected." The good memories dissipated. "It was a nightmare. Dante and my father were pressuring me to spend time with their chosen groom, Leo Girardi. He was the oldest son of another Mafia family. My father believed our marriage would seal a lifelong alliance."

Mason's mouth became pinched, and his gaze could have cut through metal. "You mentioned your parents wanted you to marry a family friend."

"That was Leo. I went on a few dates with him long before I met you. We were never engaged. In fact, I didn't spend a significant amount of time in New Jersey after that first summer. I flew in for holidays, but I made sure I had summer internships lined up after that. When I graduated, I was supposed to return home. I defied them. I had already been offered a full-time position with Family Connections."

"The private foster agency where you worked."

"I had interned with them the summer before my senior year, and I saw the director's heart and passion for the kids. I liked everything about their process, and I was thrilled to be an official member of the team."

"You miss it."

"I do. I can't explain how it felt when we made a successful placement. Knowing that hurting kids were going to a loving home, to live with people who'd been trained and equipped to help them adjust and thrive, gave me purpose." She lifted one shoulder. "On the other hand, I feel blessed to have a daughter to raise. I can't imagine life without Lily."

His unreadable gaze shifted to the board. "How long before Dante demanded your return?"

"A year. Dante started sending threatening emails

and texts. I tried to reason with him. He didn't want me around, not really. Why not let Fran marry Leo? The only reason he didn't come for me sooner was because Father's health was failing. Dante had to establish his authority in his place. By then, you and I were together." Her chest became tight. "I couldn't leave you. I wouldn't have…"

There was a knock on the door. Sighing, Mason strode over and yanked it open. "Yes?"

Candace didn't look the least bit abashed for interrupting them. "Lily wants a snack. Mind if I get something from the vending machine?"

Mason looked at Tessa. "Is that okay with you?"

"Of course."

He left the door ajar, a sign he was done rehashing the past. "The hardware store opens in an hour. I need to buy a new window. Cruz volunteered to be our lookout today."

"You have loyal friends."

"The best a guy could ask for."

Mason joined the other officers, and Tessa went to the break room. Not surprisingly, Candace didn't stick around for long. When it was time to leave, Silver and Cruz walked with them to Mason's truck and waited until they were buckled in. Cruz got into his personal vehicle, a beat-up Jeep Wrangler. Silver let them out of the gate and waved them off.

Conversation was sparse during the short ride to the edge of town, where Benson's Hardware was located. She and Lily remained in the truck and Cruz in his Jeep while Mason shopped. He emerged twenty minutes later with the window.

"We're fortunate they had it in stock. A trip down to Maryville wouldn't be ideal."

"How much was it? I'll repay you."

Backing out of the space, he shot her an incredulous look. "No way."

"Replacing your window is the right thing to do."

"I appreciate the offer, but I'm not taking your money. In fact, once this is over, we'll have to sit down and have a long chat. I plan to support her."

Anxiety stung her like a thousand fire ants. Would he take her to court and attempt to get full custody? Worse still, would he try to keep Tessa's visits to a minimum?

She averted her face and tried to push aside those worries. Mason had always been a fair person. She had to believe he hadn't changed in that aspect.

They left the hardware store behind and passed several touristy shops. One in particular held special memories.

"The Village Tinker is still in business?"

"I go in there at least once a week for fudge."

She studied his profile. She missed his smile, his laugh, his good opinion of her.

"Rocky road?"

He glanced over. "It's the best."

"You never even tried butter pecan," she protested, falling easily into their friendly argument over the confection.

"I didn't have to. I know what I like." His focus shifted to the rearview mirror, and he tensed. "We've got company."

In the reflection, she saw an Escalade speeding through the curves and bearing down on Cruz. Before Mason could call his friend, a loud popping sound reverberated off the steep terrain that hugged the right side of the road. The Jeep swerved and sped toward the rocky, earthen barrier. Tessa gasped, certain Cruz was going to smash his vehicle head-on.

"Mommy?" Lily tossed her book on the seat and tried to look out the rear window.

Cruz righted the Jeep at the last second, but it wobbled and flipped onto its side, skidding along the asphalt. Tessa clapped her hand over her mouth.

Mason barked instructions into his phone, clearly in contact with police dispatch. He gunned the engine, taking the turns at increasing speeds. His truck was in good condition, but it wasn't made to handle curves.

Lily began to cry, her soft whimpers making Mason's face harden to stone. He slammed on the brakes and jerked the truck onto a skinny side road almost hidden by trees. Tessa reached back to hold Lily's hand. When she did so, she saw the SUV gaining on them.

"Mason."

"I know."

The dense woods thinned on their right. Through the gaps, a rain-swollen river gushed over jagged rocks and fallen logs. The truck bounced over an old wooden bridge. Lily's cries grew louder.

Beyond the bridge, the trees gave way to a sloping, grassy bank. The Escalade slammed into the truck's rear corner, sending it skidding.

"Hold on," Mason yelled, forearms bulging as he fought the wheel.

They were jolted again, and this time there was no correcting their trajectory. The truck bumped and careened down the bank. Tessa braced her hands on the dashboard. She held her breath.

The roiling, greenish brown water rushed at them, swallowing the hood and battering the windshield. They were either going to be swept downstream or shot by Dante's minions.

SIX

A bullet demolished his driver's-side mirror. The river slammed his side of the truck, the water level reaching almost to his window. The force was such that he couldn't get his door open. He used the arm controls to roll his and Tessa's windows down.

"I'm going to draw them away." Mason unholstered his Glock. He'd counted the driver and one passenger. Only one SUV was present, suggesting Dante had remained in his hiding spot and sent half his team after them. "Get her out of that seat and stay down!"

Tessa unbuckled her belt and, twisting around, reached into the back seat and began to unfasten Lily's restraints. "Shouldn't we try to get to shore?"

Another bullet whizzed by and dug into his hood. They were aiming at him. Good.

He eyed the water's movement, the churning currents fed by recent rains. If Tessa slipped on a rock or accidentally let go of Lily…

Out of the corner of his eye, he saw the passenger get out of the vehicle. The short, stocky one with a mustache Tessa had identified as James.

"Backup is on its way," Mason said. "Just sit tight."

Praying that was the right advice, he leaned his upper

body out of the open window and got off a shot. James scampered to the opposite side, using the Escalade's bulk for cover. Mason lurched into the water and sucked in his breath. Icy needles pricked his exposed skin. Staying low while also keeping his pistol dry, he fought the current, his sodden boots and pants weighing him down.

The driver remained in the vehicle, but James released a volley of shots, so close he could feel the spray as they skimmed the water. He leaped onto the bank. Going up on his elbows, he got off his own shots. Glass shattered.

Mason began crawling along the bank, away from the truck. A hail of gunfire followed him, as he'd hoped. Where was backup? He prayed Cruz wasn't harmed.

He kept an eye on his truck. From this angle, it looked secure. Leaving Tessa and Lily hadn't been his first choice. If Dante and his other guards showed up, there'd be nothing Mason could do to stop them from taking the girls. Worse would be a stray bullet finding either of them.

He couldn't hear the reassuring sound of sirens above his own thundering heart, along with the river surging between its banks and successive gun blasts.

A flash of black between the trees and the flare of a well-tuned engine heralded his partner's arrival. The men noticed, too, and James slid into the SUV. They raced past Mason, headed in the opposite direction.

Mason should've waited until he was certain they were gone. Instead, he jumped to his feet and sprinted for the truck. Silver beat him there, wading into the water and scooping Lily into his arms. Tessa climbed out of the passenger-side window unassisted. She took a single step toward the bank. Silver shifted Lily to the crook of one arm and held out his other hand. Their fingers brushed. Tessa's feet were swept out from beneath her, and she lost her balance. A cry pierced the air before she disappeared beneath the water.

Everything inside him rebelled. "Tessa!"

He blew past Silver and, resetting the safety, left his pistol on a rock. The churning river tossed her as if she was in a giant washtub, pushing her mercilessly along. Tessa resurfaced, searching for something—anything—to grab hold of. He ran along the bank, gauging the terrain, hoping to guide her to an outlying rock or fallen log to hang on to. Ahead, the woods took over.

But that option was no longer viable, so Mason waded in. The water was deep, cold and menacing. If he wasn't careful, he'd wind up in need of rescue, too. He used the current to his advantage, adding his own strokes to buoy himself closer to her.

She was sucked under again, and his own lungs spasmed.

He pushed harder, resisting the urge to try to find purchase on the rocks.

Ahead, he saw her head pop up. Her body slammed into a car-sized boulder. Her fingers scraped along the uneven surface, scrabbling to grasp anything. She wasn't successful in stopping her forward progression, but it bought precious seconds.

Mason brought his boots down and leveraged himself toward her. Tessa extended her arm. He snapped his hand around her wrist like a handcuff and refused to let go.

The river swept them farther along. Debilitating cold seeped into his bones.

"Over there!" Tessa pointed to where the river curved, and massive tree roots were exposed in the bank's edge.

Mason steered them both toward the tree. As the water became shallower, his hand scraped along the bottom. He hardly registered the tiny cuts and gouges on his palm.

Together, they half swam, half limped the remaining feet to safety. They collapsed onto the sliver of rocky dirt beside the tree, lungs heaving and muscles trembling. Overhead, the sky was a delicate blue traced with wispy clouds.

Mason sat up and threaded his wet hair off his forehead, then scanned Tessa for obvious injuries. Her hair was plastered to her head, and her lips were nearly blue. "You scared me."

She opened her eyes. "*You* were scared? I'm not sure I would've made it if you hadn't jumped in."

Groaning, she pushed herself into a seated position. That's when he noticed the blood trickling down her cheek.

"You're bleeding." Gingerly moving aside the sopping tendrils, he exposed a deep gash near her temple.

"How bad is it?"

"You'll need antibiotic cream and possibly stitches."

"It could've been worse." Her gaze darkened. "You put your life at risk."

"I couldn't let you drown."

"I meant drawing the gunfire to you. Dante wants you out of the way. No sense making it easier for him."

"He's not going to get what he wants. Not this time."

Mason's fingers were featherlight where he held her hair away from the gash. His face was close enough for her to see the tiny droplets shimmering on his skin.

"Do you remember when we hiked to Laurel Falls and I sprained my ankle? You carried me on your back all the way down to our car." He'd been patient and attentive, and hadn't complained once.

Shared memories and old feelings shimmered between them.

"Yeah, I remember." Pulling his hand away, he thrust his fingers through his hair and left it in spiky tufts. He got to his feet and held out his hand. "Silver will come after us if we don't return soon."

Tessa gladly accepted his hand. She was beginning to feel the aftershocks of an acute adrenaline rush. Her legs were like gummy candy left in the hot sun too long. Thanks to the cloudy day and her cold, wet clothes, she was beginning to shiver.

Mason held tightly to her hand, just as he had in the water. Her rising panic had dissipated the moment he'd latched on to her.

"Do you think someone has reached Cruz by now?" she asked.

"Yes."

Whether that someone would help or harm was the question. Dante hadn't participated in this attack, leaving them to guess his whereabouts.

"What are you going to do for a vehicle?" she asked.

"Drive a unit truck until I can deal with insurance and go to the dealership."

"I'm sorry—"

"Don't apologize." The pressure on her hand increased, and he shot her a sideways glance. "You're not responsible for Dante's choices."

Back at the site, Mason retrieved his gun from where he'd left it. A pair of Serenity PD officers had arrived, their cruiser lights flashing. Lily was seated in the passenger seat of Silver's Corvette. The door was open, and when she spotted Tessa, she scrambled out and ran to her. Tessa plastered on a reassuring smile, crouched down and ruffled her hair. Lily looped her arms around her neck.

Silver gave them a once-over and wrinkled his nose. "I'd offer you a ride home, but neither of you are coming near my car." His gaze snagged on her, and he frowned. "Tessa, should I summon an EMT?"

Her hair hid her head wound, so he must've seen traces of blood on her face. "As long as Mason has a first-aid kit at home, I'm good."

Mason studied her. "Are you sure that's wise? You took a beating in there."

"Positive. I've got scrapes and bruises, the same as you."

He rolled the hem of his shirt and tried to squeeze the excess water from the material. "Any word from Cruz?"

"He texted a few minutes ago," Silver replied. "He's going to the hospital to get his wrist examined. His Jeep is toast."

"That Jeep was a gift from his grandfather."

"Maybe it can be salvaged."

Mason turned to survey his half-submerged truck. "I've got to get our phones out of there. Lily's car seat, too."

"I'll give you a hand," Silver said.

While the men retrieved their belongings, the officers blocked the road and informed her the crime-scene unit was en route. Officer Bell showed up and offered to take them to the station, where they could pick up Tessa's Toyota. No trackers had been found. Bell would then follow them to Mason's, where he'd help sweep the property. Silver volunteered to stand watch the rest of the day until Raven could relieve him.

As soon as they were cleared to enter Mason's house, Silver ordered them to change while he rustled up something to eat for Lily. A hot shower chased away the river's chill and soothed Tessa's aches and pains. Her lingering anxiety was another story. By coming to Serenity and seeking help, she'd put more people in danger—innocent people who were important to Mason.

Her worries must've been written on her face. When he appeared at her bedroom door with a first-aid kit, his countenance immediately clouded.

"What's the matter? Is your head hurting? I knew you should've gone to the hospital."

"I'm fine." At his disbelieving stare, she added, "Physically, I'm fine."

He gestured to the patterned armchair in the corner, angled to take advantage of the window view. "Let's get your wound tended."

She got comfortable and knotted her hands in her lap as he placed the box on the stamp-sized side table and rifled through the contents. He smelled wonderful, like a pine-filled meadow in spring. He looked better than wonderful—better than all her lonely imaginings. He'd changed into another pair of worn-in jeans and a Great Smoky Mountains shirt. The sunflower-yellow cotton was the perfect foil for his brown hair and eyes. If only she had the right to caress his cheek, smooth his hair, hold his hand…

She wove her fingers more tightly together. "How long have you been with the mounted police?"

"I joined about six months after we broke up."

Funny, she didn't recall an actual breakup. He'd just disappeared without a word, and she'd had to deal with it.

"You were content with patrol. Why the change?"

"The opportunity came up, and I craved a challenge." He gently shifted her hair, his gaze intent on her wound. "I don't see any debris in there. Can you hold your hair out of the way?"

"That's good, because I don't relish the idea of you

digging for any." Tessa hid a wince when he smeared on ointment with a Q-tip. The bruised flesh was tender.

"Sorry." His breath fanned over her forehead. "I'm afraid you're going to have a scar."

"My hair will cover it."

He straightened. "It's not too late to take you to the hospital. Or a walk-in clinic, at least. It's a deep cut."

"No, thanks."

"Afraid of needles?"

She thought of the epidural procedure and shuddered. How she'd longed to have Mason with her, holding her hand and coaching her. He was such a strong, calming presence.

"I avoid them when possible."

He opened a large bandage and positioned it with care. "We'll have to keep an eye on it. If there are any signs of infection, you won't have a choice but to be seen."

"What about your hands? I saw some cuts earlier."

He held them up. "Nothing serious."

She pointed to one in the groove of his palm. "That one could use a bandage." She stood and moved out of the way, then pointed to the chair. "Switch places."

"Yes, ma'am." Mason sat down and balanced his hand on his knee.

Tessa swabbed the same ointment he'd used onto the worst of his cuts. "Silver was working patrol in Knox-ville when I was living here. When did he decide to join this unit?"

"About a year after me. He sold his place there and bought land in Serenity. Raven joined around the same time. One officer retired and another transferred to the Nashville unit, so we had two positions to fill."

She searched the box for a small bandage. "Is Raven from here?"

"She and I went to high school together. She's several years younger, though."

She picked out a bandage, then ripped off the paper and pressed it into place. "Cruz moved here from Texas?"

He nodded. "We got approval to add a fourth officer, and he was the most qualified applicant."

Tessa closed the box. "You all seem to get along."

"Considering how much time we spend together, I count that as a blessing." He pushed out of the chair. "The horses are our partners, too. I've grown to love working with them. And being on horseback lets me interact with the community on a deeper level."

She gave him a tentative smile. "I'm happy for you, Mason. You have a nice home. A satisfying work environment. Friends and family who love you."

Although he'd said there wasn't a significant other in his life, she couldn't help wondering if he'd had any serious relationships. The thought made her slightly ill, which wasn't fair. He deserved to be happy, to be loved and adored. Preferably by someone without dangerous ties to organized crime.

"Did you have a support network in Georgia?"

"I became close with several women in my neighborhood. I also made friends at church. The women I worked with at the day-care program were genuine and kind. However, I couldn't forget I was a fraud. I couldn't forget for a moment that I was being hunted."

"Did you—" He started to sidestep her. "Never mind."

She put a forestalling hand on his biceps. "Did I what?"

"It's none of my business."

"You want to know if I dated?"

A muscle in his jaw ticked. "Like I said, none of my business."

"No, I didn't."

His gaze was skeptical. "Why not?"

"I had Lily to raise. She's my priority."

"Plenty of single parents manage to balance their children's needs with their own."

"Are you upset that I didn't have someone in my life?"

His mouth tightened. "I didn't say that."

Did he want her to confess that he'd ruined her for other men? That the mere thought of dating made her break out in a cold sweat?

"All the excitement this morning has made me hungry," he said, brushing past her and stalking over to the door. "Let's go see what Silver thinks qualifies as a healthy meal for our daughter."

Tessa nodded, relieved he'd taken some of the tension with him. She breathed in air not scented with his skin and reminded herself that reconciliation wasn't the goal. Their own hurt and disappointment couldn't get in the way of protecting Lily.

SEVEN

Mason was startled awake sometime in the night. He snagged his phone and fired off a text to Raven, who was outside patrolling the perimeter.

All good?

He got a thumbs-up emoji in response. The coiled tension inside slowly uncoiled. Then she sent him another text.

Are you in the kitchen? Light's on.

No. I'll check on it.

Shoving out of bed, he crossed to the door and opened it. He heard the rough slide of the rickety silverware drawer and the suctioning sound of the fridge door being pulled open. A high-pitched voice was followed by a shushing sound. After confirming the guest bedroom was unoccupied, he padded down the stairs in his T-shirt and pajama pants.

He found Tessa at the counter emptying chocolate

packets into mugs. His sudden appearance startled her, and she knocked one into the sink.

"Mason, I'm sorry we woke you," she said in a hushed voice. Her curls were a soft, disheveled cloud around her face. She was as beautiful as ever, and he was tempted to pull her into his arms and kiss her.

Lily rushed over to him. "I had a bad dream."

He crouched to her level and pushed a curl off her forehead. "Hot chocolate is the best cure."

Tessa was using a paper towel to wipe up the spilled powder. "I hope you don't mind. I found the box in your pantry."

"Not at all. Make yourself at home."

She nodded and looked away. "Would you like some?"

"I'll fix myself coffee." It was half past two. "I'll be relieving Raven soon."

Lily yawned. She shifted closer, wrapped her arms around his neck and rested her head on his shoulder. "Do you have marshmallows?" she asked sleepily.

Tessa observed them, her worry plain. Mason could relate. What effect would this upheaval have on Lily? She was too young to understand why she'd been ripped from her familiar world and dropped in the midst of dangerous situations. He desperately wanted to tell her that he was her dad, but he wasn't sure when the right time would be.

Hugging her close, he said, "I don't have any, but they're going on the top of my grocery list."

"I like the pink and green ones."

"You'll have to tell me what else you like."

She lifted her head. Her eyes were big and dark in her pale face, and her eyelashes were thick and spiky, like his. "Pancakes and ice cream. Oranges. Grapes. Breadsticks." She rattled off a dozen other items, and Tessa hid a smile.

"That's a lot to remember. You and your mom can write everything down in the morning, okay?"

"Will you take me to Ed's?"

"Who's Ed?"

"He makes pizza."

Tessa poured milk into the mugs. "It's an Italian restaurant. We have lunch there every Sunday. Their pizza is top-notch."

"Ah. Well, we have some pretty good pizza here, too."

Lily's brow wrinkled. "Ed gives me free ice cream."

He wondered if Tessa had thought ahead to what would happen once Dante was no longer a threat. Surely, she wasn't planning to return to Georgia. But would she want to live here in Serenity? This was his hometown. As a law-enforcement officer, he was widely known. She might not feel welcome or comfortable here, especially once the gossip mills latched on to the fact he had a surprise daughter.

His phone buzzed. "Raven's heading inside." He relayed the text. "I've got to go upstairs and change."

He patted Lily's back and stood. After setting the coffee machine to brew, he hurried to his room and changed into black cargo pants and a long-sleeved dark cotton shirt. Back downstairs, he sat at the table and began lacing up the old pair of utility boots he'd dug out of the closet when Raven entered the kitchen.

"Coffee's brewing," he told her. "Want some?"

She took in the scene and shook her head. Tessa offered her hot chocolate, which she also declined.

"I brought water." Unzipping a bag she'd left on the counter, she took out a bottle and twisted the lid open. "I'm going to bunk on the couch. Good night."

"There's an extra guest bedroom upstairs," he said to her retreating back.

"This is fine."

Tessa's gaze trailed after the female officer. When she switched her attention to him, he read the concern in the hazel depths. Putting others at risk was a problem for her. When she'd headed for Serenity, she hadn't known she would be dealing with his entire unit.

The bathroom door closed, and the sink faucet turned on.

"Lily and I will take our hot chocolate to the bedroom so we don't keep her awake."

"Raven operates on very little sleep."

Her eyebrows met. "Oh."

"She lost someone close to her, and now she says nights are her enemy."

"I'm sorry to hear that."

"Do me a favor and don't let on that you know. It's a sensitive subject."

"I understand."

She watched as he slid his service weapon into the security holster attached to his utility belt. He double-checked that he had spare ammo and a full case of pepper spray. His flashlight battery was low, though, and his backup batteries were at the stables.

"What about you and the others? Your job requires quick decisions. I don't like to think about you working on limited sleep."

"It's true this job demands a lot—physically, mentally and emotionally. We're trained to deal with a number of stressors, lack of sleep being one of them."

Mason cooled his coffee with milk and guzzled it before heading for the door.

"Be careful, Mason."

The simple words hauled him into the past. He'd worked second shift then, so they'd spent afternoons together. Before he'd headed to work, she'd framed his face and kissed him sweetly on the lips, bidding him to be careful. Without fail.

His hand on the knob, he didn't turn around. He didn't want her to see how hard this was. Having her around, in his home no less, was cracking the ice around his heart and releasing memories that seared him.

With a nod, he let himself out of the house, making sure to engage the lock. The air had a distinct chill, not unusual for April in the mountains. The half-moon bathed the trees in filmy light, enough that he wouldn't need his flashlight for most of the route he'd take around the property. He headed past the shed and leaped over the stream, which was rippling and gurgling along its shallow path.

He stopped and turned to observe the house. The kitchen light winked off, and he pictured Tessa and Lily navigating the stairs, anticipating their chocolate treat. When he'd bought the place last year, he'd known it was too big for one person. He'd hoped that one day he would meet someone to make him forget Tessa. That wasn't a fair expectation. Maybe that's why he hadn't had more than a handful of casual dates. He couldn't come to a relationship with an open heart and mind. Now that Tessa had barged back into his life, he was even less optimistic about his ability to move beyond the past.

The light from their bedroom spilled into the night. Finding that one person to share his life with was no longer important. He had a child to raise. He would focus on making up for the years he'd lost.

As Mason parked the borrowed unit truck close to the stables early Monday morning, Tessa recognized the willowy brunette hovering in the entrance.

Her stomach dropped. "Your mom is here."

He killed the engine and removed the keys. "I meant to prepare you. She called right after my alarm went off this morning. Candace apparently wasn't acting like herself yesterday, and Mom gathered it had something to do with my absence at church."

"She knows everything?"

"Yes."

Tessa mentally braced herself. Mason wasn't the only person affected by her decisions. His mom, Gia, and Candace must've believed, like him, that she'd been unfaithful. Her innocence on that charge didn't negate the fact she'd kept Lily a secret. She had hurt Mason, plain and simple. She deserved their anger and recriminations. And she would bear them, because of Lily. If she had any say, her daughter wouldn't have ties to Tessa's family. Gia and Candace would have to fill the void. It was too much to hope that Tessa could also claim that benefit.

Mason unbuckled his seat belt. "You can't blame her for being impatient to meet her only grandchild."

Tessa winced at the reproach in his voice. "Of course not. I want Gia and Candace to form a strong bond with her."

He flicked a glance in the rearview mirror. Lily was subdued this morning, content to look through her books.

"That won't happen if you go back to Georgia," he asserted in a low voice. "If you try and take her away again, you'll be in for a fight."

Tessa's head reared back. Mason's jaw was hard, his body stiff.

"I wouldn't do that to you."

He searched her face, picking away at her with his fierce gaze, leaving her sore and exposed. Their present interactions in no way resembled what used to be. He hadn't spoken to her in anger, hadn't directed his frustration at her. Unlike the men in her family, Mason had treated her with a fond regard, underscored with respect. As their bond had grown stronger, fondness had deepened into something more, something rare and precious. She had believed they would be together forever.

But then he'd lost faith in her. And in the midst of her crisis, she'd run away from him instead of to him. Time wouldn't heal their wounds, and it made her feel like giving up.

"Are we gonna see the horses?"

Lily's voice sliced through the thick, tension-choked air. Mason's chest expanded on a ragged sigh, and he pulled the door handle, popping open the door. "There's someone I'd like for you to meet first."

Mason walked with Lily, her tiny hand in his large one, and Tessa followed a few steps behind. The smells of hay, earth and horseflesh washed over her. She could hear companionable chatter and activity in the central stable area.

"Lily, this is my mom. Her name is Gia."

Gia's eyes were suspiciously bright and eclipsed only by her smile. "Hello, Lily."

Lily shifted closer to Mason and leaned against his leg. Tessa's heart fluttered. That she had taken to him so readily made this transition easier for everyone.

"She didn't get a good night's rest," he informed Gia.

Gia's forehead creased. "Poor darling. I'm not surprised, all things considered."

Mason ushered them into the break room and closed the door. "I wish we could've met at my place or yours, but it's not safe. In fact, you should have an officer escort you home."

Gia finally looked at Tessa. "Mason told me about your troubles. You did the right thing coming here. He's the best person to offer you protection. If there's anything I can do to help, let me know."

Tessa's white-knuckled grip on the plastic chair loosened. She'd expected to be blasted or berated. The school nurse was a confident woman, someone who could handle whatever life threw at her with poise. Tessa had quickly grown to admire her fortitude. Mason thought Gia was too quick to speak her mind, but that trait was balanced by her fairness and generosity of spirit. She was also a fabulous cook. Mason and Tessa had enjoyed many Sunday-evening suppers in her home. Candace had been there, too, and it had been the closest to normal Tessa had ever experienced.

Gia had approved of their relationship, but she'd let them know they needed God as their foundation. Tessa wished now she'd heeded the other woman's wise advice. Her troubles had eventually driven her straight into God's arms, however. She didn't regret that part of her past.

Silver knocked on the door and, poking his head in, addressed Mason. "We've got a lead."

Tessa would've liked to go with him, but Lily reached for her, clearly not in the mood to be left with a stranger.

Tessa dropped into a chair and pulled Lily onto her lap. Gia settled on the opposite side of the table and clasped her hands on the smooth top. The ceiling lights shimmered over her brilliant gold-and-diamond wedding ring set that Mason said she'd refused to take off, no matter how many years had passed since her husband's death.

Her brown gaze soaked in everything Lily. "She's a beautiful child."

"I know my decisions don't make sense to you."

"I am hurt," she admitted. "And shocked. I didn't see this coming."

"I owe you an apology."

"Mason explained the initial misunderstanding between you two and why you didn't seek him out." Her gaze was full of compassion. "I was a single mother for most of Mason and Candace's teen years. I worked hard to create a safe, loving environment for them. I can imagine the fear and uncertainty you grappled with. If I had been in your shoes, I might've made the same choice." The creases at the corners of her eyes became more pronounced. "My son changed after you left. There was a long stretch of time when I wondered if he'd ever recover. This unit, the horses and training, brought him back to life. I won't lie—I'm worried how your reappearance will impact him. I can't bear to see him suffer again."

"That's the last thing I want, Gia."

Before the other woman could respond, Tessa's phone rang. She fished it out of her purse and frowned at the unknown number. She chose not to answer. Instead of a voice mail, a text came through. A photo of a couple she didn't know, tied and gagged.

Her throat closed up.

"What's wrong?" Gia said.

A second text came through. Answer my call, darling sister.

Shoving the chair away from the table, she lowered Lily to the floor. The phone began to ring. A video-chat request, no less.

"Lily, I need for you to stay with Gia for a few minutes."

"But, Mommy—"

Gia stood. "Is it okay if I show her the horses?"

Tessa nodded her assent before hurrying into the hall and bursting into the conference-style office they'd used the day before. Mason was there with Silver, Officer Bell and a deputy.

"Dante's calling. He has hostages, I think. I have to answer."

Mason surged out of his chair and strode over.

She swiped the screen and was greeted by her brother's deceptively serene face. "What have you done, Dante?"

"Is that any way to greet your only brother?" he chided, his smile at odds with the glitter in his black eyes.

"How did you get my number?"

He shrugged. "I had Jorge fly down to Georgia and search your house. You really should go paperless, Tessa."

"Who are those people?"

"The Pascals? They're my reluctant hosts." He began walking through what looked like a cabin. The rustic furniture and decorative nods to black bears and the mountains told her he was nearby. The view flipped to reveal the couple in the photo. "Say hello to my sister. Oh, I forgot, you're indisposed."

The man and woman were both fair-haired. They were strapped to dining chairs and seated side by side. Gags prevented them from speaking, but their eyes broadcast their terror. Blood trickled along the man's temple.

They looked like nice people. Somewhere, there were family members who loved them. Perhaps children and grandchildren. They were in danger through no fault of their own.

"Please don't hurt them." She started trembling from head to toe.

Mason's hand came to rest on her lower back, his fingers curving around her waist.

"I'll let them live if you agree to turn yourself over to me."

She'd known that was coming. Sticky, slimy dread wound through her.

"Okay. I'll do it."

"That's not going to happen," Mason growled. Reaching up, he twisted the phone so that Dante could see him. "You're not going to lay another hand on Tessa."

Dante's smile was cold enough to freeze a mountain waterfall in summer. "Sergeant Reed, I can't say it's a pleasure to speak with you again. Let me get this straight—you're saying Tessa's life is more important than these people's?" Turning the video on them, he said, "Did you hear that? Local law enforcement isn't willing to save you. You should've chosen another place to vacation."

There was movement and a sudden, charged blast. The woman's muffled screams stabbed Tessa. The man's face contorted as blood formed a blossoming stain on his thigh.

Beside her, Mason went rigid. Around the table, Silver and the others jumped to their feet, ready to respond.

"You've made your point," Tessa gasped. "Where and when? Tell me, and I'll meet you."

"Noon. I'll text you the location right before." His mouth became an ugly slash. "And, Tessa, bring my niece."

The call ended. A terrible silence descended.

"You're not going to him," Mason declared, his eyes flinty.

"Those people are in danger because of me."

"You're not sacrificing yourself. I won't allow it."

EIGHT

Mason could feel the other officers' surprise. His customary equanimity had splintered. And no wonder. Tessa had just offered herself in trade.

"What other option do I have?" she cried, her voice quaking. "That man will die for sure if I don't, and the woman, too. Dante will shoot her out of spite."

"What about Lily?"

Her hands fisted. "He can't have her."

"I meant would you leave her without a mother? And when he realizes she's not with you, what will he do to the Pascals then?"

Silver edged past the other officers. "That name sounds familiar. Show me the photo?"

She pulled up the text and let him peruse it. "The angle doesn't show any defining architectural features."

"You think this could be one of your cabins?" Mason said.

"It's possible."

Mason tried to get a handle on his emotions while his partner contacted his assistant.

"Lindsey, I need you to check the rental roster and tell me if we have anyone by the name of Pascal." His forehead crimped, and his gray hair slid into his eyes. He flicked it away impatiently. "Their wedding anniversary? You told me last week?" Silver paced the narrow distance between the door and the table. "I *do* listen to you. How else would I have recognized the name?"

Tessa leaned into Mason. "He has cabins?"

"About forty," he murmured. "Scattered across two counties. Some are in Serenity, but the majority are in Pigeon Forge and Gatlinburg."

Silver ended the call and scowled. "Lindsey is being her usual irascible self. Did you know she accused me of taking her for granted?"

"The Pascals?" Mason prompted.

"I was right. They're a last-minute booking. Florida residents here celebrating their anniversary." He shifted past them and wrote the Serenity address on the board. "Deputy Stark, we have three hours until the meetup with Dante. Is that enough time for SWAT to organize?"

"It'll have to be." He left the room already issuing instructions into the phone.

"You plan to ambush Dante and his men?" Tessa asked doubtfully.

"We'll have the element of surprise on our side. He doesn't know we're aware of his location."

Officer Bell rubbed his hands together. "Weiland and I will provide support."

"Our unit will be there," Mason said. "In case we have runners."

Lieutenant Hatmaker wasn't going to be pleased with this new development. Like any other reasonable law-enforcement officer, he disliked bad press, anything that called Serenity PD's competency into question. Hatmaker took it a step further, however. In his mind, they were in competition with other departments to be the best, to be above reproach, to be infallible. He sometimes forgot he was dealing with human beings in police uniforms. Perfection was unattainable.

When Bell and Silver left the room, Tessa made a soft appeal. "Are you sure you have to go?"

"That cabin is surrounded by forest. Our horses can access areas patrol cars and the SWAT armored vehicle can't."

"I have a bad feeling about this."

"If everything goes according to plan, your brother and his goons will be in custody before lunch. Cruz can stay behind with you."

It was the best option. Cruz's wrist had been badly sprained. Chasing criminals through the mountains would pose a threat to his recovery. He could fire a weapon if necessary, though.

"I'm in charge of this unit," he explained. "I can't knowingly send them into danger without me."

She crossed her arms over her middle. "I pray Mr. Pascal survives."

Tessa discussing prayer in any format was unusual. Mason took comfort knowing they shared a common faith in God. That was one positive that had come out of their breakup.

He squeezed her shoulder. "I'll join you in that prayer."

Mason left her to find Cruz and make his request. The officer was already in the locker room getting ready to suit up. He wouldn't have chosen to be left out of the action, but he agreed that watching over Tessa and Lily was the best option.

"Thanks, Cruz."

"I'm happy to do it."

Mason, Silver and Raven worked quickly to get their horses loaded into the trailers. His mom insisted on remaining at the stables. Tessa didn't seem to mind, so he didn't argue the point.

When the others were in the truck and ready to go, he crouched before Lily. He finally understood what officers with wives and kids went through. His chosen career posed significant risks. Even a routine traffic stop could prove deadly.

"Can I have a hug, ladybug?" He'd heard Tessa using the nickname, and it rolled off his tongue with ease.

She wrapped her arms around his neck. "Are you going to ride Scout?"

"I am."

"I gave him an apple. He's my friend."

"I'm sure he liked that." He smiled and lightly tapped her nose. "I'll see you in a little while." Standing, he turned to Tessa. "I'll call you with an update as soon as I can."

She looked so anxious he almost offered her a hug.

Cruz gave him a thumbs-up as he left the building. Mason climbed behind the wheel, and they began the twenty-minute ride through twisting, mountainous roads. They were in almost constant contact with Bell and Deputy Stark. SWAT was estimated to arrive in another half hour. Because the mounted police were playing a support role, they would take care not to let their presence be detected.

Silver got on the phone with Lindsey again and verified that the property next door to the Pascals' rental was unoccupied. The land parcels were large and wooded. Mason turned into the specified driveway and parked the truck at the far end, using the generous, three-story structure to further obscure their presence.

As they unloaded the horses and rechecked their gear, Mason had to work at maintaining his composure. That frustrated him. His equine partner, Scout, depended on him. His human partners did, too. They depended on each other. They were a cohesive team, and if he let himself be distracted, he could make a mistake that could cost someone their life.

Officers Bell and Weiland arrived mere minutes before SWAT. The highly efficient team fanned out across the property next door and got into position. Silver had sent them floor plans of the multilevel luxury cabin earlier, so they'd have time to plan. Silver, Raven and Mason mounted their horses and remained on standby.

Minutes ticked past. The temperature was pushing seventy-five degrees, and his uniform absorbed the sun like a sponge. Sweat trickled between his shoulder blades.

He glanced over at Silver, who wore his long-sleeved uniform shirt and gloves. How the guy managed to look as cool as a Popsicle he had no idea.

The woods were a serene vista. The smell of a charcoal grill and sizzling beef carried on the breeze. When would the sounds of invasion break the spell?

Scout's flesh rippled with tension. Mason's anxiety was leaking into his horse and making him antsy.

Raven cocked her head, listening. "Either this is the most peaceful takeover ever or we got the wrong address."

Silver cocked a brow. "Lindsey make a mistake? Not likely."

Bell's voice crackled over their radios, letting them know he was returning. They watched for his familiar form on the road. He jogged the length of the driveway.

"They're gone," he said, panting. "Dante must've had someone watching the stables and was informed of our visit."

"The Pascals?" Raven demanded.

"Inside. The woman's unharmed. We have an ambulance on the way for Mr. Pascal."

Mason was on the verge of splintering apart. "He's going after Tessa."

Silver reached over and took Scout's lead. "Go."

The instant his boots hit the ground, he began sprinting for the cruiser. "You and me, Bell."

The other officer did an about-face and hurried after him.

How long of a head start had Dante had? They hadn't encountered the SUVs on the drive up the mountain, but side roads were plentiful. Once seated in the passenger seat, he called Cruz.

Bell buckled in and started the engine. "Anything?"

"Voice mail."

"That doesn't mean he's in trouble."

Mason punched in Tessa's number. Then his mom's. No response from either of them.

Bell took the curves at excess speeds. "Remember, cell signal is spotty in these mountains."

He gritted his teeth hard enough to make his jaw ache. His mom, Tessa and Lily were sitting ducks. What if they didn't reach them in time?

Tessa paced the length of the aisle. Three horses observed her from their stalls. The past hour and fifteen minutes had crawled past. Why hadn't Mason reached out?

"I'm going to speak to Cruz," she announced, stopping short.

Gia waved her on. "Go ahead. Lily and I will keep Iggy company."

Iggy, a good-humored quarter horse, was enjoying the

attention. Tessa wished the majestic creature could distract her from the constant wondering and worry.

God has this under control, remember? Worrying won't change the outcome. You have to trust His plan.

Tessa strode to the short, broad hallway where the break room and offices were located. Cruz was in the smallest office, seated at the lone desk, and was watching the security feeds. One camera was angled at the main entrance and parking lot. The other showed the paddock.

He looked up at her approach. A purple bruise on his chin was the only indication, other than his bandaged wrist, that he'd been in an accident. "I haven't had any updates."

She sagged against the doorjamb. "Shouldn't we have heard something by now?"

Rubbing his hand over his short black hair, he leaned back in the swivel chair. "Not necessarily. Every case is different. SWAT is running the operation, not us. Now, if the perps leave the cabin for the forest, Mason and the others will pursue them. That could take a while. Besides, cell reception isn't reliable in these mountains."

If Mason was in trouble, he might not be able to get a message to her.

Cruz gave her a sympathetic smile. "Mason doesn't take unnecessary risks. He's a professional."

"I believe you." What no one else seemed to want to believe was that Dante shouldn't be underestimated.

Cruz's gaze returned to the cameras, and he shot upright in the chair.

"What is it?"

"We've got company," he said intently, nodding to the man using pliers to snap the gate's lock. One Cadillac was waiting behind him. "You, Gia and Lily—get to the tack room and don't come out."

He ushered her out of the office. When she hesitated, waiting instead to watch him test the front-door lock, he urged her to hurry.

Tessa tamped down her rising horror and rushed into the center of the building. Gia immediately noticed something was off.

"We have a situation," she said, trying to keep her voice even. Scooping up Lily, she beckoned for the other woman to follow. Gia didn't ask questions. Nor did she comment when Cruz stormed past and used a key to unlock a cabinet stocked with weapons. Tessa regretted not learning how to use a gun. Then she could have helped the officer instead of leaving him to defend the stables alone.

Gia entered the long, narrow, windowless room first. Tessa closed the door behind her and searched for something to block it.

"It smells, Mommy."

Lily wiggled to get down. Tessa released her and followed her to the far corner, where Gia was standing, her hands clasped at her waist. The lines around her mouth were more pronounced.

"Cruz has some police business to take care of, and he asked us to wait here. I'd like to pray for the police officers who work to keep us safe. Want to join me?"

Lily took her hand and held out her other one to Gia, who didn't bother hiding her surprise.

"I think that's a great idea," Gia murmured, her voice choked with emotion.

Tessa offered a prayer for safety without giving details that would alarm Lily. God knew them, anyway. Lily went second. Her prayer was very brief, as usual, and precious. While Gia was praying, the muted sound of gunfire and splintering glass greeted them. Her hold on Tessa's hand tightened.

The door was rammed open, the thick wood thudding against the wall shelving. Tessa spun around and shielded the others.

"Bruno!"

The loyal Vitale employee hadn't changed much over the course of four years. He was still a bull of a man, with massive fists that could break a person's face.

"Don't make this harder than it has to be," he said, holstering his gun.

"Bruno, please. I have a daughter now." She backed up, and Lily grabbed onto her legs. "Dante is like a son to you, right? You would do anything to protect him. I can't let you have her. But I'll go willingly with you."

Gia made a noise of protest. Bruno didn't spare her a glance as he advanced into the room. Like Dante, this man didn't know the meaning of compassion.

"Dante wants you both."

Tessa glanced around, desperate to stop him. She seized a pitchfork and wielded it in front of her. Lily began to cry softly.

Bruno stopped. A vein in his neck bulged. Sighing, he took out his gun again and aimed it at Gia.

"Put it down, Tessa, or she dies."

"Don't, Tessa," Gia said softly, sadly.

Shifting in front of Gia, she glared at him. "Put the gun away."

"You first." He gestured to the pitchfork.

Her stomach in knots, she let it fall to the floor.

"Come over here," he ordered.

Tessa reached down and, easing Lily's hands free, gently pushed her toward Gia. "I love you, ladybug."

When Lily almost lurched forward, Gia wrapped her arms around her and held her fast.

"Mommy!"

Her heart splintering, Tessa approached Bruno. His mitt-sized hand latched on to her upper arm. The blast of gunfire coming from the main entrance told her Cruz was being kept busy with the other goons.

"Let the child go," he said.

"No!" Tessa tried to shove him out the door. "I said I'd go with you. He's not getting anywhere near her!"

He didn't budge, just trained the gun on Gia. When Gia didn't react, he jammed the barrel into Tessa's skull.

"This one's death certificate is already signed. You insist on being stubborn, and you shorten her life."

Her mouth opened, and her gaze snapped to Tessa's, apology and tears filling the brown depths. She let go of Lily, who shot across the room to hold on to Tessa.

Bruno scooped her up as if she weighed nothing, lodged her beneath one arm and pushed Tessa through the door. She stumbled, and he caught her in a bruising grip, forcing her toward the side entrance.

"Stop!" Cruz's command volleyed down the aisle. She managed to look over her shoulder. He was crouched inside one of the empty stalls, his weapon ready.

But he wouldn't take a shot, not with Tessa and Lily in the way. Frustration was carved into his face.

Bruno marched into the lane between the stables and the paddock. Bright sunshine hampered her view. She tried to think of a solution. If she fought back, Bruno or one of the others would likely shoot her and take Lily.

Her vision cleared enough for her to make out the waiting Cadillac, angled close to the building. Another one was idling on a side street beyond the paddock, where her brother was no doubt watching. The blood in her veins threatened to dry up as their unwanted reunion loomed. Would he take his time killing her, or would he show her mercy?

The crunch of boots on gravel behind them was accompanied by a sharp command. Mason and Bell emerged from the stand of trees edging the paddock. At the same time, Cruz eased out of the building, his weapon aimed at Bruno.

"You're not leaving here with them," Mason said with steely calm. His gaze didn't flicker to her or Lily, and his expression was a closed book.

Bruno's fingers dug into her flesh. He whirled, his head swiveling to take in all the officers. In the distance, the second SUV peeled out and disappeared onto a secondary road.

Bell spoke into his radio and set the deputies on Dante's trail.

Mason continued to edge closer. "You're outgunned. There's no reason for this to get ugly."

The driver shot at Cruz, who dove to the ground. Bruno released her. Tessa's hands closed over Lily, who was screaming at the top of her lungs. To her relief, the much larger man didn't fight her. He pounded after the vehicle.

Tessa scooped Lily into her arms and ran for shelter. A shot rang out, followed by a grunt and a thud. Tires screamed against the pavement.

There was a scuffle. Tessa didn't wait around to see the outcome. She entered the stables, believing they'd be safe, when strong arms closed around her like a vise.

NINE

"Thank the Lord you're okay," Mason breathed, his lips catching her hair. His heart thundered against his ribs.

Tessa melted against his chest, her arm coming around his waist, fingers tangling with his utility belt. Tremors worked through her body. Her breathing was ragged.

He would've been content to hold her all day, or at least until they'd both recovered from that close call. Lily had other ideas. Plus, his mom wanted to see for herself that no one was harmed.

"Oh, Tessa, I'm so sorry," she gasped, taking her hands. "I didn't know what to do."

"It's okay."

"What happened exactly?" Mason asked, dreading the answer.

His mom launched into a detailed explanation. "Tessa was very brave."

Mason couldn't speak. He hated it when violence was visited upon innocent civilians, much less people close to him.

"How did you know to come back?" Tessa asked, tucking Lily close to her side.

"Dante figured out our plans. When we got there, they were gone."

Had he ordered one of his goons to surveil the stables? Had he hacked Tessa's phone and listened in to their conversations? Although that would take serious skill, Dante had the means to make it happen.

"The Pascals are being taken to the hospital," he informed them. "I'll call and get an update later. We'll go home soon." It was nearing lunchtime. While he was new to this dad business, he'd already learned that Lily benefited from frequent and timely meals. "Stay inside while I check on things."

Mason walked outside in time to see Bruno being loaded into an ambulance. The deputies would accompany him to the hospital and stay there until he was ready to be transferred to the county jail.

Cruz ambled over. "You guys got here in the nick of time. I almost lost control of the situation."

Meaning, Tessa and Lily almost got taken on his watch. "Leaving you alone was my call. What happened falls squarely on my shoulders." He gestured to the building. "How are the horses?"

"Spooked, but okay. I'll show you the damage to the building."

They walked around to the front, where Mason assessed the busted gate lock and the obliterated main entrance. Fixing that was a priority.

"I'll take care of all this," Cruz said. "Go be with your family. They've had a traumatic morning."

He didn't correct Cruz. Tessa wasn't technically family. As the mother of his child, however, she was automatically in his circle of important people.

When Raven and Silver returned, he helped them unload Scout, Lightning and Thorn, and settle them inside. Silver left to meet Lindsey at the cabin and determine if there had been any property damage. Raven and Cruz would remain at the stables and oversee the necessary repairs. Officer Weiland agreed to accompany Mason and the others to his home. Before they left, Mason called around to several alarm companies and found one available to install a system in his home that day.

His mom asked to spend the afternoon with them. She might be as tough as nails, but this was enough to rattle anyone. They had a quiet lunch in the kitchen with the curtains drawn. Afterward, his mom volunteered to show Lily how to bake cookies. He recognized the attempt to distract the little girl and appreciated it. If he wasn't preoccupied with the escalating threat, he would've participated.

Mason found Tessa on the screened-in porch. Seated with her back to the wall, staring at nothing in particular, her fingertips slowly polishing the mug's surface, she looked fragile and hollow. The opposite was true, he knew.

She looked over at him. "I know I'm not supposed to be out here. I just needed five minutes of fresh air, blue sky and birds singing."

Of normalcy. A reminder that there was good in the world. "I get it." He pulled out the chair next to her and sat. The screen across from them still bore evidence of the henchman's bullet. "Bell just got here. He and Weiland are at the end of the driveway. The alarm company should be here any minute."

"A cost you weren't planning on."

"It's worth it. I hope you understand about your phone. Let me know if you need to make any calls while you're waiting to get it back." He'd given the phone to Deputy Stark. Their department was larger and had the capabilities to determine if it had been compromised. "You're welcome to use my laptop anytime."

"Anything that will help prevent another scene like today, I fully support. Any updates from the hospital?"

"Mr. Pascal is out of surgery and is expected to make a full recovery. Silver has already pledged to refund their rental fees and travel expenses. He'll also cover any out-of-pocket medical expenses."

"I'm sad their memories of East Tennessee are tainted. At least they survived." She swallowed hard. "What about Bruno?"

"No need for surgery. The bullet went clean through his shoulder."

"Bruno is important to Dante. I don't know how he'll react to him being taken into custody."

"The sheriff's department has increased security."

"They won't get any information out of him," she warned.

Mason nodded in deference to her personal knowledge. "It's one less man to contend with. Maybe rattling Dante is a good thing. He'll be more likely to make a mistake."

"Or do something rash." Her eyes were twin tombs. "I don't want to contemplate how Lily will be treated if he were to take her to New Jersey. His hatred for me would bleed into that relationship. My sister betrayed me, so I have no hope she'd stick up for my child." Her fingers latched on to his arm, and she crowded his space. "No matter what happens to me, promise you'll move heaven and earth to keep her out of his clutches."

His mom's words scrolled through his mind. Bruno had said Tessa's death certificate was already signed. Figurative words, of course, but no less chilling. When he'd come out of those trees and seen her and Lily seconds away from being ripped from him, Mason had been desperate to save them both.

As if of their own volition, his fingers slowly and reverently traced a line from the bandage on her temple to her jaw. Her eyes flared with surprise. Beneath that, he recognized loneliness and longing.

She'd been alone for so long, shouldering explosive secrets. He'd been alone, too, and not because he relished the bachelor life. Because she'd taken away his right to decide.

Tessa must've sensed the shift in his mood, because she lowered her gaze and removed her hand from his arm.

"I don't want you to worry," he said gruffly. "Lily's well-being is my top priority." Scooting out his chair, he said, "We should go inside."

Tessa still loved him.

That first year without him had been a nightmare. The fear that Dante would track her down. The worry about her unborn child and how ongoing stress would impact the pregnancy. The separation from Mason— missing him, aching to see him, talk to him, hold him. When she'd brought their daughter into the world without him, she'd made a conscious choice. No more mourning what she'd lost. She had to pour all her energy into raising Lily and creating as normal a childhood as possible. Out of a need for self-preservation, she'd buried her love for Mason.

Those moments with Bruno, when it seemed she would soon be reunited with her brother, she'd released the lock on her feelings. She'd allowed herself to fully feel again. Why wouldn't she cherish what they'd shared if she was on her way to die?

But she hadn't died. Mason had rescued her. And he had held her so tightly and tenderly. Just now, he'd caressed her face and regarded her with affection. Like old times.

What did it gain her, though? Fresh hurt. Fresh pain. Fresh rejection. Not because of Dante's actions, but her own.

Certain she couldn't keep her turmoil hidden, she murmured an excuse to him and Gia and slipped upstairs. In the privacy of the bedroom, she poured out her heartache to Jesus and took comfort in the Scriptures' promises. God loved her. He wouldn't leave or forsake her.

Tessa was physically and mentally spent. When Gia brought a sleepy Lily upstairs, Tessa opted to take a nap, too. The sound of a vehicle woke her more than two hours later. She left Lily tucked beneath the blankets and padded downstairs. Through the living-room window, she watched the security company van get swallowed by the trees as it disappeared down the drive.

"Feel better?"

Tessa finger-combed her hair off her forehead and gave Gia a perfunctory smile. "I will after I've had a cup of coffee."

"I just made a pot."

Gia poured a cup for Tessa and retrieved the milk from the fridge. She then returned to her cutting board and continued dicing onions and tomatoes. The curtains were drawn, and needles of sunlight poked around the edges.

"I'm not usually a nap taker," Tessa said, sipping the rich brew. The house was silent, and she wondered what Mason was doing. "Has the security company already installed the system?"

She nodded. "He was quick and efficient. He will have to come back later and do the upstairs windows. Mason wouldn't let him disturb you and Lily."

"Oh."

"After what you've both been through, you've earned the rest."

"Thank you for entertaining Lily. Actually, I've been meaning to find someone to teach her to bake."

A genuine smile curved her lips. "She's a delightful child. You've done an excellent job with her."

Her cheeks heated. "Thank you. I had support from the community."

"You made friends, I hope?"

"At first, I kept people at a distance. But when my pregnancy became apparent, women in my neighborhood started popping by unannounced. They brought me books, maternity clothes and baked goods. I blame my weight gain on Barbara Roland's caramel brownies." She smiled, remembering how Barb and the others had become her tribe. She wondered if she'd ever see them again.

Gia's gaze flicked past her shoulder. "Are you going to stand there all day or are you going to help me make salsa?"

Tessa didn't need to turn around. Her stomach flip-flopped as Mason slowly traversed the room and came to a stop beside her. How much had he heard? She glanced at him, relieved to see his expression wasn't shuttered like before.

She glanced down at her wrinkled scoop-neck shirt and pants, wishing she'd taken a moment to change before coming downstairs. Her hair was no doubt in wild disarray, the default hairstyle she'd been born with.

"Was anyone with you during the delivery?" he said, washing his hands and retrieving an extra knife and cutting board.

"Lisa, my next-door neighbor, is a pediatric nurse. She volunteered, and I accepted."

As he diced the vegetables, his movements were both careful and precise. He had tanned, strong hands, thick wrists and corded forearms. His watch face caught and refracted the overhead light as he worked. Tessa was reminded of the countless meals they'd prepared together, sometimes just the two of them and sometimes with Gia and Candace.

"Were there any complications?"

"None."

Tessa got the feeling he wanted to ask more pointed questions but refrained. Later, when the time was right, she'd give him the opportunity to delve more deeply into Lily's birth.

Gia's perceptive gaze bounced between them. "Tell me about how you came to be a believer, Tessa."

"I was a regular patron at the library, both before and after Lily's arrival. Mrs. Smith, the head librarian, invited me to church. I was both fascinated and confounded by her faith. She talked about God like He was a dear friend. It was a natural thing for her to bring Him into daily conversations." Her father and Dante thought believers were weak. "My circumstances drove me to a place where I was in desperate need of peace, and I eventually recognized God was the true source. I also had much to be forgiven for, and it comforted me to know He was willing and able to forgive me."

Gia swiped at her eyes. "These onions," she muttered.

They shared a smile that buoyed her spirits. She felt Mason's gaze on her.

"I'm happy you had a support system," he said. "More important, I'm happy you found God."

"When did it happen for you?"

"A year or so after we broke up." His spiky lashes

swept down to hide his eyes. "I pretty much hit rock bottom."

Now *she* was ready to cry. At least she'd had Lily to focus on. "That must've been hard."

"Hard for this mom to watch." Gia's voice was raspy.

"Good came out of it," he pointed out. "I'm a changed man."

Lily's wobbly voice called for Tessa.

Mason immediately put down the knife. "Do you mind if I go?"

"Of course not."

He quickly washed his hands and went upstairs. Tessa set aside her coffee and took his place at the cutting board.

"He's enamored with her," Gia noted fondly. "He's talked about having children off and on through the years."

"He'll be a wonderful father."

Reaching across the counter, she squeezed Tessa's hand. "God will see you through this, Tessa. He brought you, Mason and Lily together for a reason."

Without faith, it is impossible to please God. That was one of the first verses she'd memorized, and she'd repeated it to herself whenever fear threatened to overtake her. Now that Dante knew her whereabouts and was launching an all-out campaign to ruin her, fear was her greatest enemy.

He wasn't just gunning for her anymore, either. Mason was in his crosshairs.

TEN

Mason was in his study that night fielding texts from his sister when Tessa came searching for him. He waved her in and offered her a seat. Instead, she hovered by the door.

"Am I interrupting?"

He placed his phone on the desk. "Candace wants details about what happened this morning." She was nosy and pushy, but he couldn't imagine life without her.

"She's right to be worried about you."

"She's worried about all of us. My guess is she's also jealous that Mom got to spend the day with Lily, and she didn't."

Her lips curved into a semblance of a smile. "Lily's asleep. I didn't think she'd be tired after her long nap, but these last few days have been chaotic."

"I've heard Candace say that kids like routine, especially at that age."

As a brand-new father of a three-year-old, he felt at a distinct disadvantage. He had little experience with kids, and the amount of knowledge he needed to do this right was overwhelming.

"Gia was really helpful today. I'm glad she came over."

He was glad, too, because her presence had been a buffer. It bothered him how quickly he'd gone from anger and distrust to awareness and yearning. He couldn't afford to be attracted to Tessa, because he couldn't continue to throw up barricades. They were co-parents of an innocent, vulnerable child. A team. He had to treat her as a friend, not an enemy.

"Do you mind if I use your washer and dryer in the morning?" She pinched the material of her wrinkled shirt and pulled it away from her body. "I didn't bring many clothes with me."

"Of course not. Use whatever you need." Her disheveled appearance didn't detract from her soft, inviting presence. She took his breath away, no matter what she wore or how her hair was styled. "If you think of anything you'd like from the store, let me know."

"Thank you." Tessa gestured to his open laptop. "Anything new?"

"Bruno is settled in at the county jail. He'll be in the medical area until he's ready for general population. Raven renewed her efforts to warn area residents."

"I'm afraid the Pascals aren't the only ones who will be hurt by him."

He shared the same concern. "We've got a lot of people working on this."

She pulled a flash drive from her pocket. "I thought you might want to see Lily's baby pictures. I keep copies on my computer, so you're welcome to keep this."

"Thank you." Mason immediately inserted it into his laptop.

"I'll say good-night then." She turned to go.

"Why don't you stay?" he blurted. At her raised brows, he said, "You can give me a running commentary."

She hesitated. "If you're sure…"

He reached out with his foot, hooked the chair leg and

tugged it closer. She sat down and clasped her hands in her lap.

The first photo knocked him back. Wearing a soft pink, flowing dress, Tessa was pictured outside a brick building with budding dogwoods all around. Her smile was wide, teeth showing, her eyes dancing at the camera. Her curls had been tamed into an elaborate, upswept style. His gaze zeroed in on her bulging stomach.

"I forgot about this one," she said quickly. Leaning across him, she would've clicked the next photo if he hadn't seized her wrist. She froze, and he did, too.

Her bones were delicate beneath his fingertips, her skin as soft as he remembered. Her hair tickled his chin as she angled her face toward him.

He allowed his gaze to roam her features—features he hadn't been able to oust from his mind. The sweeping, elegant eyebrows, the earnest, intelligent eyes, the straight nose and full lips.

His mouth went dry. His hearing dulled until he could only detect the *pound*, *thud*, *pound* of his heart.

He wanted to kiss her. He *longed* to kiss her.

"I can't."

Her brows slapped together. "Can't what?" she whispered.

Oops. He hadn't meant to say that aloud. Instantly, he released her and shifted away. "Nothing. Ah, how far along were you in this photo? Where was it taken?"

She audibly swallowed and left his personal space. "I was about seven months. Lisa, my neighbor, also attends the same church. She talked me into splurging on this dress, and she insisted on taking my photo after service that day. For Lily's sake."

He stared at the screen. "You look radiant."

"I didn't feel anything other than awkward, but thanks."

Mason moved on to the next one, and was overcome for a different reason.

"She was beautiful from the start, wasn't she?" Tessa murmured. "She weighed seven pounds and three ounces at birth."

"She didn't have much hair."

A light trill of laughter filled the room. "That didn't last."

They continued through dozens of pictures. Some evoked a deep, emotional charge, while others made him laugh out loud. Tessa answered his questions at length. He knew she regretted her choices and their impact on him. That didn't erase the complicated mix of emotions he was feeling. It also didn't answer a question that haunted him—if she could go back in time, would she make the same choices?

When his phone buzzed, he noticed the late hour and the caller's identity at the same time.

"What's up, Silver?"

"We have a problem."

Mason listened to his explanation with growing unrest. As soon as the call ended, he answered Tessa's unasked question.

"Bruno escaped."

"What? How?"

"Silver's not sure of the exact details. We know that two prison employees have been hospitalized. The jail is on lockdown until they review footage and complete the investigation."

Tessa buried her face in her hands. He twisted in his chair and cupped her shoulders.

"It's an unfortunate setback, but we have dozens of men searching for them. Who knows? This could all be over tonight."

ELEVEN

At first, Mason thought the alarm pulsing through the dark house meant someone had triggered the new system. He was reaching for his pistol when he smelled smoke.

Bolting out of bed, he quickly dressed, tucked his weapon in his rear waistband and tried unsuccessfully to get Weiland on the phone. The door wasn't hot to the touch. He entered the hallway and immediately started choking. Wispy fingers of smoke licked at the ceiling.

Dropping to all fours, he crawled toward the stairs and yelled Tessa's name. Where had the fire originated? Why wasn't Weiland answering?

When he reached the stair railing, a wall of heat slammed into him, sucking the breath from his lungs and drenching him in sweat. Irate flames ate at his front door.

His sense of urgency intensifying, he bellowed for Tessa. He inhaled acrid smoke, and his voice disintegrated into hacking coughs. Going on his belly, he crawled military-style, feeling as if he was clambering through mud. Another bout of coughing stalled him.

Why hadn't the shrieking alarm roused them?

Their bedroom door loomed before him. What would he find behind the wooden barrier?

Mason lunged for the knob and twisted. Complete

darkness greeted him. He flicked the light switch and got nothing.

"Tessa?" He hurried toward the bed. "Wake up!"

As his eyes adjusted, he saw that the bed was empty. Had to be a trick of the shadows. He swept his arm across the mattress.

Denial rose in his throat. She wouldn't have left on her own, wouldn't have left him to burn inside this house.

The curtain at the window rippled, admitting a shaft of fresh air. Open. The window was open. His hands gripping the sill, he leaned out and scanned the yard. The movement activated the battery-operated security light, and his stomach dropped at the sight of the industrial ladder in the grass.

Dante had come for them.

He thought he heard screaming. If he didn't figure out a way to get out of this house, Tessa would soon be dead and his daughter would be in the Mafia prince's clutches. Getting her back through legal means might be impossible, thanks to Dante's influence.

Mason searched the house's exterior for anything he could use to climb down. Finding nothing, he returned to the hallway, only to double over when his lungs seized. The smoke had thickened. He couldn't go down the stairs. Couldn't get to the ground from Tessa's room.

What now?

Dear God, help me so I can help them.

Tessa struggled against her captor's rock-hard grip. A few steps ahead, James had Lily wedged against his shoulder like a slab of beef. Her arms were outstretched toward Tessa, and her fear-filled cries startled birds from their homes as they passed under the branches. His high-beam flashlight sliced through the trees and underbrush, lighting the path, but it wouldn't catch the attention of Officer Weiland. She'd seen his prone body beside his cruiser. She didn't know whether he was merely unconscious, or worse.

Mason wasn't coming, either. She managed to twist enough and get a glimpse of the farmhouse. The upstairs windows were black, sightless eyes, and orange-yellow flames flickered in the first-level windows like an evil, mocking smile. The tacos Gia had made for supper threatened to come up.

"Mason!" The anguished cry got her nothing but mocking laughter.

"He's a goner," her captor sneered, jerking her over the uneven ground. "And you will be soon. You deserve it after all the trouble you've caused the boss."

Tears threatened, and she blinked them away. Grief wasn't her friend. Right now, she had to focus on escape. Her life depended on it.

"Where are you taking us? Where's my brother?"

The vise on her arm became punishing, and she tried to pry his fingers loose. The goon, who was well over six feet, stopped short, hauled her against him and captured her other arm. She tugged and pulled, but to no avail. His crude laughter washed over her, even as his grip became crueler. Any second now, she expected to hear her bones snap.

"We're wasting time, Vince," James called without stopping. "The fire department will be here soon."

Vince brought his face close to hers. "Not in time to save Sergeant Reed," he taunted.

She kicked him square in the shins, and he growled his displeasure. "If it had been up to me, I would've made his death a lot messier. Like yours is gonna be."

"Let's go." James's command cracked the night.

Vince's cruel eyes bored into hers a beat longer, then he started dragging her at a punishing pace.

Defeat was inevitable. She was no match for these men. How was she supposed to get herself and Lily free?

Her heart beat out a rhythm of regret. Tessa hadn't wanted to admit that escaping Dante was out of the question. No one escaped his wrath, not forever.

A two-lane road dissected the woods. Waiting there was a different vehicle, an older Suburban in place of the Escalades. No sign of Dante, Bruno or the fourth guard.

Tessa balked. This couldn't be the outcome.

"Let me hold her," Tessa called to James. "I can calm her. You don't want to present an out-of-control child to Dante, do you?"

He stopped beside the rear door and turned around, considering. Lily whimpered and squirmed. Tessa's body vibrated with adrenaline. Should she run once she had Lily in her arms? Was it worth the risk to them both?

Vince surprised her by agreeing. "You're driving, James, and I'm not wrangling that sniveling brat on the way."

"Fine. Get in." James opened the door and pointed to the row seat. The dome light spilled onto the ground. Lily's round face was mottled, her lashes drenched with tears. "Then I'll give her to you."

Tessa's only opportunity shriveled, and so did her heart.

I failed to keep our daughter safe, Mason. I'm so sorry.

Vince yanked her forward. In the next second, the iron grip on her arm fell away. A gasp stirred the air. He hit the ground in a quivering, contorted form. Tasered. By whom?

Out of the shadows, a figure in black emerged.

Joy and relief crashed over her. Mason had gotten

out. He'd come for them, their very own personal hero. *Thank You, Jesus.*

He looked ferocious and unpredictable, with his hair in wild disarray, his features obscured by soot and his hands wielding a Taser and a pistol. Lily's crying resumed, and Tessa saw James mentally run through his options. Any second now, he was going to use Lily as a shield or a bargaining chip. She didn't think, just acted.

Screaming out her rage and fear, she charged and grabbed Lily's waist. Startled by the outburst, James let go. Tessa ran for the trees on the opposite side of the road, a good distance from the guns but still within view of Mason.

A single shot reverberated through the night, and she flinched. Mason dove to the ground. The Suburban's engine rumbled, and tires spun out. Mason discharged his weapon but failed to disable the fleeing vehicle.

Tessa remained where she was as he bent to check the prone man's pulse. Clearly finding none, he stalked across the road, his boots beating out a furious rhythm, his body as rigid as a flaming arrow. She involuntarily took a step back even as he wrapped his arms around them both, his careful embrace at odds with the emotions he held in check.

Little by little, she rested against him, taking solace in his unsteady heartbeat and heaving breaths. He reeked of smoke, but she didn't care.

"You're angry."

"Yes."

"At me?"

"What?" His hands cupped her upper arms, and he eased back to look at her. "No, of course not."

His voice sounded terrible, like he'd inhaled a sack of burning embers.

"I couldn't warn you. When I woke up, one of them—James—was already climbing onto the ladder with Lily, and the other one had a gun. He ordered me outside. I—I had to stay with her. And I know what I did just now was risky, but I couldn't stop myself. I just knew he was going to toss her into the back and drive away."

"I'm not angry, Tess." He cradled her cheek, his thumb sweeping over her cheekbone. "I've been operating on the assumption that I was going to be too late." He ceased speaking and took a moment to gather his thoughts. "I'm proud of you. You kept your cool. Didn't panic. Not many people in your predicament could've done that."

Tessa wanted him to hold her again, but he turned toward the road. "James shot and killed his partner rather than deliver him into our custody."

"His name was Vince. Maybe they didn't want to risk another jailbreak?" She felt terrible about the loss of life, despite his ill intentions toward them. "I saw Weiland. I think he's dead."

"I checked on him. They knocked him unconscious. He'll have a nasty headache, but he should be fine."

Mason dissolved into a fit of coughing. Tessa stood by, feeling helpless.

"You have to go to the hospital."

He straightened. "I'm okay."

"How did you get out?"

"When I discovered you and Lily were gone, I made my way back to my room and climbed out onto the porch roof. I shimmied down a column and used the railing as a foothold. I heard Lily crying and figured you all were in the woods, so I decided to try and cut you off via the road."

Sirens alerted them to the first responders' impending arrival. They made their way back to the driveway entrance and were met by Weiland. He was upright, using the car as a prop, but obviously in pain.

The stench of burning wood carried through the trees, and Tessa could see the orange-yellow flames dancing with glee. Before she could dwell too long on Mason's enormous loss, the fire trucks and ambulances rolled in, trailed by Silver and Cruz. Mason would've led them to the slain man, but Silver witnessed him have another bout of coughing and ordered him into a waiting ambulance.

"We'll take care of this," Silver reassured him, no trace of his usual droll wit. "And I'll personally see that Tessa and Lily are kept safe."

An EMT was already at Mason's side.

Mason gave her a half-hearted wave. "I'll text you."

"I don't have a phone."

"Right." He winced. "I'll contact Silver as soon as I can."

She watched as he was led to the nearest ambulance. Firefighters were swarming the scene, shouting commands to each other and working to save the house. If it could be saved. Lieutenant Polk and some other officers arrived, and Silver quickly consulted him and Cruz. He then retrieved the car seat from the borrowed unit truck and hustled Tessa and Lily to his car.

"Where are we going?" she asked.

"I would take you to my place, but I'm in the middle of renovations. Lots of dust and tools that make it unfit for a toddler." The engine purred, and he maneuvered the Corvette onto the dark road. "I have an unoccupied cabin that is isolated and accessed by a single lane. Easy to defend."

The dashboard clock glowed. Half past three. "My presence is seriously messing with your unit's sleeping habits."

Not to mention putting them in harm's way and causing destruction to their private property. Even their workplace hadn't gone untouched. She swallowed down rising panic.

"We need to be tested sometimes," he said, maneuvering a sharp turn with ease. "Pushed to our limits. Besides, I like the adrenaline rush."

He flashed a lopsided grin, and she could see how Serenity's female population could be dazzled. Since first meeting him, Tessa had sensed that his flippancy was a deflection technique. Mason wouldn't betray his friend's secrets, however, and she didn't know Silver well enough to pry.

The smooth ride lulled her into an exhausted silence. She couldn't keep track of the turns and twists as they climbed higher into the mountains. There were fewer residences here. Finally, he turned onto a wooded lane that led to a single cabin shrouded in darkness. The absence of trees behind it, coupled with an ocean of twinkling stars, suggested they were on top of the world. Their only neighbors would be black bears and other wildlife.

Silver told her to stay put while he went through flipping on lights. Satisfied, he escorted her and a half-asleep Lily inside and told her to pick a room. He'd be bunking on the couch. Cruz would be there later and could take one of the other four rooms. The place was both grand and welcoming, with high ceilings and wooden beams overhead, a stunning stone fireplace, floor-to-ceiling windows and plush throw rugs. She had no doubt it would be spectacular in daylight. Right now, she wanted nothing but sleep.

Tessa chose the master suite. Once she got Lily tucked beneath the comforter, she ducked out to the living room. Silver was lounging at the kitchen bar, typing into his phone. He had fingerless gloves on tonight. Less formal than the ones he wore with his police uniform, they were a soft tan material. His long-sleeved cotton shirt came over the gloves so that not even a strip of skin showed.

He looked up at her, and she knew that he knew what she was thinking. His unusual violet eyes seemed to dare her to put voice to her questions. Then, his lips quirked in that typical grin.

"I've just had a text from Mason. He's at the hospital waiting to be seen. Not patiently, I might add."

She rested on the couch's fat arm. "I don't know how long he was trapped in the house."

"He's going to be fine. You all are."

"His house was set on fire because of me."

"Not you." He set his phone on the counter and faced her. "Your brother."

"Details."

"Mason has his priorities straight. He values people above anything else. Trust me, he's not thinking about what he's lost tonight. He's thinking about what he didn't."

Mason didn't leave the hospital until late Tuesday afternoon and the doctors were satisfied the oxygen delivered by mask was enough. He'd argued against having a tube stuck down his throat, especially since his chest X-ray and blood work were normal. They gave him a sack of inhalers and pain meds and made him promise to return if he experienced shortness of breath.

Raven picked him up and drove him to Silver's cabin refuge in the sky. He bid her goodbye and climbed the steep steps, surprised when he experienced a bout of light-headedness. He paused at the top and sucked in air, then winced. The inside of his throat felt as if he'd swallowed needles.

Silver answered his knock with a lift of his pale brows. "They didn't let you shower?"

"I was hooked up to oxygen all day." He detested feeling weak, especially now. "Where's Tessa?"

He probed the interior for a sign of her or Lily. He'd been here once before, when his friend had first purchased it as a foreclosure. Silver had transformed the place.

"They're in the pool."

"The interior pool downstairs? I thought you were going to get rid of it."

"Lindsey argued to keep it."

If Mason hadn't felt like a strong wind could push him over, he would've interrogated his friend. Silver had a lot of first, second and occasionally third dates with a woman before moving on. He had no permanent female ties in his life, other than with his assistant. Mason had once asked if he felt anything personal for Lindsey, and he'd quickly shut him down. Theirs was a professional relationship, he'd insisted, nothing more.

"Where did they get swimsuits?"

"Lindsey went to Uncle Ollie's Outfitters. She got the suits, towels and some clothing for them both. Toiletries, too. But you three will have to do some serious replacement shopping in the next day or so."

He glanced down at his filthy clothing. "Do you have anything I can change into?"

"I've got a spare set of clothes in my car. Meanwhile, I'll throw yours in the washer."

"Thanks, brother. For everything. I've asked a lot of you in recent days."

"I'll find a way for you to repay me," he said with a grin.

Mason's quiet laugh turned into a short bout of coughing. Silver's grin was wiped clean.

"Did you leave the hospital against medical advice?"

When he could speak again, he said, "I have my discharge papers right here."

Silver returned with a cold bottle of water. "Take care of yourself, Mason. Those girls need you."

He took long, grateful chugs. "I'll be as good as new in a day or two."

"You think Dante's going to give you time to recover before he launches his next assault?"

"That's the problem. We've been playing defense too long. It's time to start canvassing local shops, bars, restaurants. You know how chatty the locals can be. Someone, somewhere, has to have seen something that can lead us to where he's holing up."

"Patrol unit can help with that. I'll also reach out to Deputy Stark. He said the sheriff's department is willing to help in whatever capacity necessary."

This wasn't the sheriff's department's case, and he appreciated their cooperation. The additional manpower was crucial, especially since he and his unit were focused on protecting Tessa.

Mason kneaded his forehead. The nurse had said his headache was caused by carbon monoxide. "I'm going to shower."

He needed to see Tessa and Lily. In the long hours inside that isolated hospital room, he'd replayed the scene with James and the now-deceased Vince. Once again, he'd almost lost them.

Silver showed him to a room separated from the others. "This cabin has two master suites. Tessa chose the other one."

Mason strode between the sitting area and fireplace and placed the sack of meds on the king-size bed. "How's she doing?"

She'd amazed him with her courage and determination, facing off against those thugs.

"She blames herself for everything that's happened." Silver leaned against the door frame. "I have a feeling she's a flight risk."

His knees gave out, and he sank onto the mattress. "She wouldn't."

"Guilt is a powerful motivator, my friend. Our current troubles, combined with your tangled past, are enough to send her packing. Have you told her that you forgive her?"

He clamped his lips together.

"Have you made sure she knows you *want* to protect her? That she made the right decision coming here?"

Mason racked his brain. Had he?

"She still loves you," he stated matter-of-factly.

Silver couldn't possibly know that. "We share a child together. Of course we care about each other's well-being."

"There's no 'of course' about it. Plenty of people who share children despise each other."

Mason couldn't feel that way about Tessa. He could be angry with her, frustrated and hurt because of what she'd done, but he could never despise her.

"We're not getting back together."

He couldn't even let his mind go there. All he could see down that route was heartache. He wouldn't be surrendering his heart to Tessa again.

TWELVE

After a long, hot shower, Mason was ready to sleep for days. Instead, he donned Silver's plain polo shirt, too-long pants, which he rolled up at the ankles, and socks, and followed feminine voices to the downstairs pool. Pausing at the glass door, he watched Tessa choose a sandwich and baby carrots from a platter, then place it on Lily's plate. The patio-style table was framed by a giant window with a view of the mountain ridges marching into the horizon. Lily was wrapped in a neon-pink-and-yellow towel, her curls in disarray and her skin flushed from her recent swim. Tessa wore a demure white wrap of some sort over her swimsuit.

Lily said something, and Tessa smiled in response. That smile was like the one she used to give him, and it made him yearn for those dreamy, uncomplicated days. Things had been easy between them then. Falling for her had been the most natural thing in the world. Who wouldn't love a woman like her? At first, he'd been attracted by her beauty and the sweetness she radiated, but he'd soon discovered her character was worth pure gold. She stood up for the weak and vulnerable and hated to see anyone suffer. If she could help someone, she did. Plain and simple. He'd been challenged by her generosity and spurred to renew his commitment to his community. Their personalities complemented each other, and it hadn't taken long for him to start thinking about spending forever with her.

Tessa glanced up, noticed him there on the other side of the door and stilled. Instantly, the strain of the past days had her in its grip. Her worry for him was written in her expressive eyes and her full, trembling mouth. Despise Tessa? Impossible. Exactly what he felt for her, he was afraid to examine. One thing he had to make clear— they were far from enemies.

He pulled open the door and was hit with a wave of humid air, heavy with chlorine. The tickle in his throat thankfully didn't progress into another coughing fit. Tessa didn't move as he walked around the pool's edge and made his way to them.

Lily grinned at him. "I got to swim!"

Mason sat in the chair beside Lily. "Maybe I can swim with you later."

"Yes, please!" She waved a carrot in the air. "Mommy, can we swim with Mason?"

He hid a grimace. Mason wanted her to know he was her father, but so far, the right opportunity hadn't presented itself.

Tessa was seated opposite him. Her gaze seeming to absorb him, as if she hadn't expected him to ever return from the hospital. Was she as tormented by flashbacks as he was? For a while last night, she'd believed him to be stuck inside his burning house, succumbing to the smoke and flames.

"Maybe we can later." She gestured to the platter. "Are you hungry? Lindsey was here earlier, and she stocked the fridge."

His stomach growled in response. "I hadn't realized I was until I sat down."

He snagged a sandwich and a canned soda, and he and Tessa ate while Lily chattered about her pony books and the library back home.

"There's a nice library here," he told her. "I'll take you there someday soon."

Her eyes brightened, and she sipped her juice. "Do they have Tillie and Toni books?"

"It's possible. If not, there's a huge bookstore over in Pigeon Forge."

Tessa's lashes swept down, and her mouth looked sad.

"It's your mom's favorite store," he informed Lily. When Tessa's head whipped up, he added, "Used to be, anyway. I took her there at least once a week. I browsed the magazines while she poured through the science-fiction section."

He met Tessa's gaze, and they simply stared at each other, remembering. Their habit was to order coffee at the in-store café, then chat for a while before going their separate ways through the store.

"Mason took me to used bookstores all over this area. No matter how far away it was, he'd take me without complaint."

"Remember the one in Tellico? We drove for hours, only to learn it had shut down months prior." He chuckled, remembering her chagrin.

"I should've done my research," she agreed wryly, rubbing at the condensation on her soda can.

"The Snack Shack we found by the river made up for it. They had the best hot dogs and fries I've ever had."

She leaned forward. "Remember that cheese dipping sauce?"

"I could've taken home a tub of that stuff." He rubbed his stomach. "I wouldn't mind eating there again."

The flush of delight showed in her twinkling eyes. "I wonder if it's still in business."

Lily dropped her carrot on her plate. "I want fries."

"Maybe I can take you to the Snack Shack someday soon."

"Mommy, too?"

He sensed Tessa's gaze on him. He'd begun to think of them as a package deal, but when this was over, he and Tessa would be parenting separately. They would have to work out a shared custody agreement. In his opinion, the best solution was for Tessa to find a place to live here in Serenity so they could both spend the maximum amount of time with Lily. But would she want that?

Honestly, the whole idea saddened him. When he'd dreamed of his own family, it hadn't looked like this. But he and Tessa had to find a way to make this work.

"Your mom is welcome to come with us."

He risked a glance at her, and she was preoccupied with her food, picking at the crust instead of eating.

"Say yes, Mommy!"

"We'll see." Tessa avoided his gaze. "For now, finish what's on your plate. Miss Lindsey brought brownies for us."

Lily's energy kept the tension at bay. After the meal, Mason and Tessa carried the leftovers upstairs. Silver was snoozing on the couch, so they quickly hustled Lily into the master suite. He would've left them to their own devices, but Lily begged him to watch a show with her.

Once Lily had changed into dry clothes, she hopped onto the bed and patted the mattress. Mason joined her, using the mound of pillows as a prop, and he settled in to watch her favorite shows on her device. He was keenly aware of Tessa seated across the room by the fireplace, flipping through a magazine. She cut a lonely figure. If they were a true family, she'd be huddled up with them. He and Tessa would pretend to be interested in the kid's cartoon while sharing secret looks. Maybe he'd tuck her hair behind her ear. Knead her tense shoulders. Tickle her palm and make her laugh.

You're not together. You can't think such things.

She had changed into jeans, flip-flops and a Smoky Mountains shirt, clearly purchased from the tourist shop. Her hair was woven into a thick braid that allowed him a clear view of her defined cheekbones, jaw and delicate ears. While he was watching, she fished out her lip balm and applied it. Did she use the same brand? The shiny kind that tasted of coconut when he kissed her?

He closed his eyes against the pain of the past.

"Are you sleeping?"

He opened his eyes and found Lily's face hovering close. Tapping her on the nose, he shook his head. "I wouldn't dream of it."

Although, now that he had a full stomach and was propped on a soft, inviting bed, the hours of sleep he'd lost were catching up with him. He made it through one half-hour episode before he had to get up or fall asleep in their room.

Pushing to his feet, he padded to the fireplace. "Can we talk?"

Tessa looked up, wariness and concern at war in her hazel eyes. "Go to bed, Mason. Whatever it is can wait until tomorrow."

"It's not even eight o'clock."

Setting aside the magazine, she stood up. "You're about to fall over. Your body needs rest."

"You'll be here in the morning, right?" he prompted, Silver's warning resurfacing.

Her brows crashed together. "I'm not going anywhere."

"Good. That's good." She was right. He needed a clear head when he told her what was on his mind. "Good night, Tess."

"Good night."

Tessa set the flour and sugar containers on the counter, then searched the lower cabinets for a mixing bowl. For a rental cabin, the kitchen was well-stocked. She was learning Silver didn't do anything halfway.

"You're up early."

Crouched and peering into the cabinet, she twisted on her heel and almost toppled over.

Although dressed in his own clothes again, scruff darkened his face and his hair was mussed. She snagged the bowl and carefully stood, aware that her heart rate had tripled—not because he'd startled her, but because he wasn't the in-control, focused, authoritative police officer right now. He was an extremely handsome man with no barriers in place...half-asleep, rumpled and approachable. She yearned to close the distance between them and snuggle into his warmth and strength.

"I, ah, couldn't sleep." She glanced out the wall of windows, where the sky was a delicate purple. "I thought I'd make pancakes. Lindsey asked for a grocery list yesterday, and she delivered. Did I disturb you?"

"No, I slept like a rock." He went to the coffeemaker, situated beside the fridge, and perused the various flavors. "I can't remember the last time I had pancakes. I usually grab some yogurt and a banana before work."

"I'm making enough for everyone." Tessa resumed her preparations, trying to ignore the magnetic pull he had on her. When they were a couple, she'd reveled in how he made her feel. She'd been free to be affectionate with him then. "Silver was already awake when I came in here. He took coffee out to the officer on duty."

He was pouring his coffee when he noticed the tin can Tessa was preparing to open.

"Beets? What...?"

"Lily likes pink pancakes. They're what make the pancakes pink."

"You can't be serious." He came to stand close beside her. "Hiding beets in a pancake? That's just wrong. The grocery store has food coloring, you know."

"This is the healthy alternative. Kids are notoriously picky. These recipes help parents sneak in nutrition. You'd be amazed at what you can hide avocado in. There's even a recipe for black-bean brownies I've been wanting to try."

"I just lost my appetite," he grunted, sipping his coffee.

"You're not even going to try them?" Her eyebrows winged up. "They're actually decent."

"Decent is not the quality I expect from my pancakes, Tessa. Mouthwatering, butter-soaked, fluffy. That's my style. That's normal breakfast food."

Smiling at his mock outrage, she dumped the beets into the blender and hit the button. She expected him to take his coffee to the seating area or possibly join the other men outside. Instead, he rounded up a skillet and spatula for her, then set out the eggs and maple syrup. It reminded her of the times they'd cooked together.

She remembered suddenly that he had wanted to talk to her, and she accidentally dropped an egg. It cracked on the polished wooden floor, the insides oozing perilously close to Mason's sock-covered feet.

He snagged several paper towels and cleaned up the mess.

She washed her hands and faced him, arms folded against a sudden chill. "Are you planning to try for full custody?"

His eyebrows hit his hairline. "Where did that come from?"

"You had something on your mind last night. After our talk about the Snack Shack, I gathered you wanted to establish alone time with Lily. I'm fine with that. What I'm not okay with is you taking her away from me."

He set down his cup with a thud. Cupping her shoulders, he looked her square in the eyes. "I'm not going to do that, Tess. You have my word."

She couldn't think with him so close, his eyes delving deep into her soul, his hands keeping her from flying apart.

"I need to ask your forgiveness," he stated thickly.

Her jaw dropped. "For what?"

"Believing your brother. Doubting you. Being stubborn and self-pitying to the point I refused to even talk to you."

Tessa couldn't stop her hands from gripping his sides, above his waist, where sleek muscle met his thick work belt. "Where did you go? I pestered your coworkers and your mom and sister for a full week. I went to the police station. Candace's day care. No one would tell me anything."

"Into the mountains. The backcountry."

"You went *camping*?"

She'd pictured him on a beach somewhere, possibly with a beautiful woman on his arm, one he'd left her for.

"Hiking through the forest alone seemed like a good escape. I didn't realize my mistake until I was out there.

I couldn't escape thoughts of you. We spent so much time together in these mountains." The skin around his eyes went tight. "Things might've been different if I'd only given you a chance to explain. I'm sorry."

"Oh, Mason, I'm sorry, too. I hate that I hurt you." A sob worked its way up her throat, and she was hard-pressed to contain it. The tears wouldn't be checked, however. They slid down her cheeks and under her chin.

He pulled her close and wrapped his arms around her. She went willingly, eagerly seeking comfort and release from the guilt that had become part of her daily existence. Mason let her cry without reservation. He was a sturdy support, tenderly caressing her back in a rhythmic, soothing motion. She wept for past mistakes, lost time and what might've been.

When her tears were spent, she lifted her head and caught him discreetly dashing moisture from his own eyes.

"We're going to be okay," he declared huskily. "We were a good team before. We'll be an even better team now because we both want what's best for our daughter."

Tessa let out a shaky breath. He wasn't insinuating that they would be a couple again. Their history was too mangled to overcome. But they could be wonderful co-parents.

The fact that she longed to frame his face and pull his mouth down to hers proved it wasn't going to be easy... not even close.

THIRTEEN

"Will we be anywhere near a grocery store?" Tessa buckled into the unit truck's passenger seat and propped her cross-body purse on her knees.

"If black beans are on your list, the answer is no."

"I'm not going to make healthy brownies, especially after you acted like my pancakes were poisoning your body."

Mason smiled, opting not to tell her they weren't as terrible as he'd pretended. He'd wound up eating those ridiculous pink pancakes in order to appease his daughter. She'd offered him some in that musical voice, her big eyes fastened on him, and he hadn't been able to refuse. Tessa had found the exchange amusing, of course. He'd made a show of adding an extra helping of maple syrup, silently daring her to comment. Her smile had only grown wider.

Mason was getting used to shared meals. While he had a standing invitation to eat at his mom's and the unit had frequent cookouts, he ate alone when at the farmhouse. He liked listening to Lily's chatter, and he liked observing how Tessa interacted with their daughter. She was a good mother—loving, patient and a pro at fending off impending meltdowns. He wouldn't have managed on his own as well as she had.

Don't forget this togetherness will end as soon as Dante is in custody. This family facade will splinter into Daddy-Lily time and Mommy-Lily time.

He couldn't allow his past feelings for Tessa to confuse matters. He was over her. Had been over her for years. Just because holding her made him feel whole again didn't mean they could pick up where they left off.

"Did you see Silver's face when I told him the ingredients?" he said.

His friend had dug in to a full stack without knowing what gave them the pink hue.

A full-bodied laugh bubbled up in her throat. "For a second there, I thought he was going to be sick." Watching the cabin grow smaller in the rearview mirror, her humor faded. "I hope leaving Lily was the right decision."

"Silver will manage just fine until my mom gets there."

Lily had very little to entertain her, and all three of them were in need of clothes. He'd decided a stop in town could be arranged, as long as they didn't linger. Officer Bell would accompany them while another officer remained to guard the cabin. First, he had to meet with the insurance adjuster and stop by the stables.

Despite having Bell as a police escort, Mason remained on the lookout for suspicious vehicles. When he turned into his driveway, his thoughts were yanked from potential threats to the destruction of his home. He left the truck without a word. Tessa did the same, remaining next to the vehicle while he slowly walked around the ruined structure. The fire chief had told him that between the fire and the water damage, it couldn't be saved. He would have to rebuild.

I know what Your Word says, Lord. You work all things together for my good. This doesn't feel good, though.

He'd poured a lot of time, energy and money into making the old farmhouse a comfortable home. His off-duty hours this past year had been dedicated to updates and repairs. His mom and sister had helped him paint the entire first floor. He'd watched countless video tutorials in order to repair the upstairs bathtub. He'd added the screened-in porch himself. All that work, for nothing.

I have no choice but to praise You, Father. You are good all the time, no matter what. You've protected us from evil. You saved us from the fire. That's what matters.

A glance around reminded him that the property itself had been the selling point, not the house. It was a gorgeous piece of land in a good location. He still had the trees, the creek and the mountain view. He could envision Lily running through the yard, a puppy yipping at her heels.

When he rejoined Tessa, her sadness was almost palpable. "Are you okay?"

"I will be." He'd work with an architect to design an even better layout, a home with his child in mind. "You know that verse about God making beauty from ashes? Lord willing, I'll have a new and improved home one of these days."

"Where will you stay until then?"

He shrugged. "I could rent a camper and stay here on the property or rent one of Silver's cabins. My mom's is an option, too."

Any response was swallowed up by the insurance agent's arrival. Again, Tessa gave him space, taking refuge in the truck cab while he and the agent discussed the next steps.

When he climbed behind the wheel, he angled toward

her. "Promise me you won't leave town. You're not alone anymore. We're going to face Dante together."

Her startled gaze slid from his to roam the damaged structure outside the windshield. Her thoughts weren't hard to decipher. He expected a tally of his losses and the close calls, the reasons why coming here had been simultaneously beneficial for her and detrimental to him. Instead, she looked at him and nodded.

"I promise."

He swallowed his hastily prepared arguments. "Good."

Officer Bell, who'd been waiting at the driveway's edge, waved as they pulled onto the road. At the stable gates, he punched in the code Cruz had messaged to him. Dante's attack had helped them identify weaknesses around the stables, and they'd responded with intensified security measures. Once he'd parked the truck, he and Tessa hurried to the front entrance and entered another code. The lock deactivated, and he pushed open the new, bulletproof glass door. Music filtered through the building, punctuated by conversation.

Cruz and Raven were grooming their horses. They both looked surprised to see him.

"I thought you were supposed to rest today," Raven chided, her long braid swinging in defiance. Her horse, Thorn, seemed to send him a baleful glare.

"Too much to do," he responded. The dip between Tessa's eyebrows deepened, and he felt compelled to explain. "The chest tightness is almost gone. I feel almost fully restored after a full night's sleep."

Her concern didn't immediately fade, and he had to admit it was nice to know she cared that much.

Hearing his voice, Scout moved to the door of his stall and whinnied. Mason greeted his partner with a hearty pat and a peppermint. Tessa asked Cruz about his wrist.

"It's mending just fine."

"What about your Jeep? Silver mentioned something about possibly being able to repair it?"

Mason turned and caught the negative shake of Cruz's head. "It was on its last legs. I'll go vehicle shopping when I get the chance."

"I need a truck. Maybe we can go together," Mason chimed in. "What's the plan for today?"

"Patrolling the square and Glory Pond," Cruz responded. "We're going to show Dante's picture around and see if we get any tips."

He prayed they received solid leads. Dante and his men would continue to spread their destruction. Mason was troubled by James's ruthless actions. Dante's goons were willing to turn on each other, and that didn't bode well for the citizens of this town.

"I may join you on patrol tomorrow." He led Scout out of his stall. The horses were used to a certain routine, and these past several days had been anything but.

"Not a good idea." Raven had that obstinate set to her chin. "You have to stay with Tessa and Lily."

As the unit's senior officer, he had the final say. He respected his fellow officers, however, and took their opinions into consideration.

"You do have a target on your back," Tessa reminded him.

He didn't like to think of the cases and other responsibilities that were taking a back seat because of his personal problems. He also felt like he owed his officers and the patrol unit, along with countless deputies, a huge debt of gratitude.

"We'll take it on a day-to-day basis."

Raven didn't have a response to that, which he accepted as agreement. She and Cruz went to the locker rooms to change, and he located his grooming tools.

"Want to help?"

Tessa eagerly accepted the curry brush and went to work while Mason gathered a bucket and muck fork. He was inside Scout's stall when Cruz poked his head in.

"We're headed out. Want us to wait for you?"

"Bell is out there. We've got to make a quick shopping run after this."

"I forgot to mention that the Houston Falls High School principal called yesterday. He had questions about Friday."

Mason had forgotten that his unit was to take part in a regional event. Various law-enforcement agencies and first responders would be on the school campus for a meet and greet with students and citizens of the community. "We'll have to skip this year."

"Skip?" Lieutenant Hatmaker's voice drew them both out of the stall. He was in uniform and had taken off his hat. Thumping it against his thigh, he stared at them in disbelief. "You can't be serious. Serenity's mounted-police unit attracts scores of interested students, teachers and parents. You bring positive press to our department. You can't skip."

Tessa stopped in midstroke and leaned into Scout's bulk, disquiet covering her features.

Raven had hold of the truck keys, and they jingled as she approached. "Are you aware that Mason's home burned down the other night?"

"I heard." He looked at Mason. "I'm sorry that happened. Were you able to save any of your belongings?"

His grip tightened on the muck rake. "I haven't gotten permission to enter yet." The fire chief was supposed to contact him. Mason held out hope that a few mementos, like family photographs and his father's Bible, could be salvaged.

"At least you survived." Hatmaker's attention flickered to Tessa. His nose pinched, as if he was annoyed by her very presence. "And since you didn't suffer life-threatening injuries, you won't have a problem fulfilling your obligations."

Cruz took a step forward, a vein bulging at his temple. "This wouldn't have anything to do with the fact that the host school's principal is your brother-in-law, would it?"

"You're out of line, Castillo."

Mason put a staying hand on Cruz's shoulder and addressed Hatmaker. "What about our Mafia problem?"

"The campus will be crawling with law enforcement. Your man would be an idiot to try something then."

Mason noticed Tessa's scowl and eye roll. She had lived with the villain and was intimately acquainted with his arrogance and audacity. But once Hatmaker settled something in his mind, it would take the force of dynamite to change his mind.

"We'll be there," he said, feeling Cruz's shoulder bunch with annoyance.

"Good." His fingers tightened on the hat. "Now that we have that squared away, how about you explain exactly how the stables came under attack. Did you sign off on the security upgrades?"

Cruz shook off Mason's hand and took a step forward. Mason grabbed his arm. "You and Raven go ahead and patrol. The horses are probably getting antsy."

His jaw clenching and unclenching, he nodded and stormed out of the building. Steam practically spewing from her ears, Raven pivoted on her heel and followed.

"Tessa, do you mind finishing up with Scout? Take all the time you need."

Mason took Hatmaker through the scenario, literally walking him through the stables and taking extra time in the tack room, emphasizing the danger to Tessa, his mom and Lily. Just as these men had no qualms hurting Mason's family, they wouldn't hesitate to hurt innocent bystanders. But Hatmaker seemed unfazed. While Mason agreed a last-minute withdrawal would be unfortunate, the potential for violence couldn't be ignored.

Before the lieutenant left, Mason broached the subject once more. "The chief is aware of our participation on Friday, I assume?"

He pulled on his hat and stared at Mason from beneath the brim. "He is aware, and he and I are in agreement. This is an event we can't afford to miss."

Schooling his features, Mason bade him goodbye and rejoined Tessa as she was returning Scout to his stall. She'd finished the mucking for him.

"He didn't change his mind, did he?" She gave Scout a final pat.

"Unfortunately, he doesn't often change his mind about things. You and Lily will have to come with me. There won't be anyone to guard the cabin. Don't worry, we'll work out a plan."

"I trust you."

Mason registered several things at once. They were alone. She was very close, and her face tilted up, her golden-green eyes wide and clear. Her lips shone with her favored gloss. Was it his imagination, or did he smell coconut?

Reaching out, he plucked straw from her hair, taking his time while doing so. The strands were fine and springy. He outlined the fresh bandage with his fingertips. "How's this healing? Any sign of infection?"

Her eyes were transfixed on his face. Was she leaning toward him? "It's, ah, fine. Just fine."

Scout chose that moment to demand attention, butting Mason's shoulder with his face. Tessa blushed and ducked her head. Mason didn't know whether to be disappointed or relieved. Relieved, his cautious mind urged. Kissing Tessa? Big mistake.

"We should go. Bell's waiting."

Without a word, she accompanied him into the overcast day. Bell was waiting in his cruiser, and he gave them a thumbs-up.

There was no traffic on the secondary street. Everything seemed serene, but he couldn't shake the feeling they were being watched. He stayed close to Tessa as he walked with her to the passenger-side door and ushered her inside.

"Mason—"

A distinct whistling pierced the air. The door window exploded. He lunged for her, shoving her down on the truck seat and shielding her with his body.

Above his frantic heartbeat, he heard Bell return fire and shout on the radio for backup.

"Mason."

He shifted the bulk of his weight onto the seat's edge, looked down and got a nasty shock.

Blood seeped through her shirt.

"You're hurt." He tugged aside her collar to inspect the damage. There was a deep wound right below her collarbone and too much blood for him to guess the cause. "Have you been shot?"

"N-no, I don't think it's a bullet wound. The pain would be worse." Her ravaged gaze snagged him. "Right?"

The volley of bullets had stopped. Staying as low as possible, he pulled the door closed and rummaged in the dash compartment. He got a fistful of fast-food napkins and pressed them against the wound. She gasped and went paler.

"I'm sorry, sweetheart. We have to slow the bleeding." He took her hand and pressed it against the napkins, which were already turning a deep crimson.

Bell brought his cruiser alongside the passenger side and rolled down his window. "You guys good here? I have to look for the shooter."

"Tessa's hurt. I'm taking her to the hospital."

"I'll follow you through the gate."

When Tessa made to sit up, he put a restraining hand on her shoulder. "Stay put."

If there was a bullet lodged inside, movement could jar it and nick a vital organ or artery. He climbed over her on shaky legs and started the engine, aware that the curvy road to the hospital would be its own nightmare. They had at least a forty-minute drive, and that was if he was doing average speed. He would have to drive below the limit in order not to jar her. But by then, she could bleed out.

Please, God, don't take her away. Lily needs her.
I'm afraid I do, too.

Tessa was lying in an awkward position, one leg bent with her ballet flat propped on the bench seat, and the other braced on the floor. Wind whipped through the busted window. Forested hills hemmed them in on either side, and she watched the trees flash past.

The searing pain around her wound site was severe, but it was limited to the surface. She could breathe unhindered, and she was alert.

"Silver, is my mom there yet?" Mason demanded in a terse tone. "Good. Keep her and Lily away from the windows, and be ready to defend the cabin. We don't know how many Dante is working with. He could've flown in more of his own people or hired local criminals."

He guided the truck through a series of tight, high turns, and Tessa's stomach cramped. She closed her eyes and inhaled the earthy, mossy air in an effort to keep the nausea at bay.

The shooter had to have been surveilling the stables and would know Lily wasn't with them. Dante could use this opportunity to try to snatch her.

Mason ended the call. "Silver will guard her with his life."

When she didn't answer, he lightly touched the top of her head. "Tessa? You with me?"

"I'm going to sit up now."

"Don't."

She grabbed the headrest and pulled herself into a seated position. The nausea intensified for a few seconds, but she closed her eyes again and willed away the panic.

"Lay back down before you pass out."

The tendons in his arms stood to attention where he gripped the wheel. His dark eyes were stark.

"These curves are making me sick," she said, keeping the napkins snugly in place. "Sitting up will help." When he started to protest, she said, "Mason, the wound site is the only part of me that hurts. I must've gotten grazed by the bullet or stray glass."

"You're still going to the hospital."

Tessa couldn't argue the wisdom of that, even though she'd rather be on the way to Silver's cabin. Being apart from Lily right now was not ideal. When anxiety threatened to overwhelm her, she started praying. God loved Lily even more than Tessa did, which was tough to wrap her mind around. He had a plan for her daughter—a future and a hope. If she didn't cling to His promises, fear would consume her.

The road evened out, and they entered a picturesque valley with emerald green fields and soaring, blue-green mountains. The smooth ridges were dotted with cabins. Campgrounds, shops and mom-and-pop restaurants welcomed visitors.

She lowered the sun visor and used the mirror to evaluate the wound. Carefully lifting the napkins, she saw that the uneven gash was no longer oozing blood.

"How bad is it?"

"Deep enough to require stitches," she sighed. "I'm not about to poke around to find out if something is embedded inside."

"We may have to postpone the hospital visit." Mason checked the side mirrors and frowned. "That sedan has been following us since the outskirts of Serenity."

"Didn't you say this two-lane road is the main link between Serenity and Pigeon Forge?"

"True, but this is a top-of-the-line Cadillac with a rental sticker. Could be nothing, but my gut's telling me otherwise."

As they approached another steep set of curves, this time headed down into the outer limits of Pigeon Forge, the sedan sped up. Tessa twisted in the seat for a better look and recognized the driver.

"That's James," she exclaimed.

He held out his phone. "Call 911. Stay on the line with them."

Tessa did as he asked, relaying pertinent information while Mason navigated the curved roads with increasingly excessive speed. Perspiration dampened her nape beneath her hair, and that sick feeling in her stomach returned.

As they came around the last kink in the road, the sedan bumped into the truck's bumper, jolting them.

Mason kept the vehicle steady. The next hit shuddered through the cab, knocking Tessa sideways into the door. The phone slipped from her fingers and sailed through the open window. She reached out in vain as the truck left the road and the tires caught on bits of gravel.

Mason jerked the truck into a hard right, careening between two ramshackle buildings onto a cracked, paved road. A billboard that was partly covered with ivy advertised a tourist attraction. A high, kudzu-choked hill hugged one side of the road. On the other, spindly trees were all that stood between the road and a deep crevice.

"I lost your phone."

"They have our last location," he responded. "This road dead-ends at an abandoned water park."

"What happens when we reach the dead end?"

Mason's gaze penetrated hers. "We ditch the truck and lose them on foot."

FOURTEEN

The property owners had erected a chain-link fence around the water park to keep out trespassers. Not to be denied, someone had used wire cutters to open a make-shift entrance, where a welcome banner and turnstiles stood. Mason punched the gas and aimed for that opening. The truck's front end split the fence wider, and the jagged metal fingers scraped like nails along the sides.

In the rearview mirror, he saw the sedan emerge into the parking area and hurtle toward them.

"Time to bail."

Slamming on the brakes, he brought the truck to a stop mere feet from the old pay booths. Tessa's seat belt dug into her wound, and she cried out. Waving off his apology, she popped the door latch and scrambled out. Mason met her at the front bumper as he unholstered his weapon. He grabbed her hand and they started running.

Instead of going straight ahead through the littered corridor that was lined with lockers and bathrooms, he led her to the left, and they darted between trees, over-grown brush and what once had been a baby pool. Brack-ish green water in the shallow basin tainted the air with a nasty stench.

Shouts sounded behind them. James had brought a friend, maybe two.

Up ahead, debris littered the cracked pavement. They were forced to slow their pace and dodge slabs of wood, probably from the half-dismantled stairs that used to lead to a lifeguard lookout. A bullet dug into the cement near his feet.

They had to find cover. It had been over a decade since he'd been to the water park, and he wracked his brain trying to remember the layout. There was an indoor pool somewhere beyond the spiraling tube slides. That could be their answer.

Tessa pointed to the cement slides ahead. "Now what?"

Woods formed a natural barrier beside the slides, and the fence was beyond that. He didn't have wire cutters and no way to know if there were other man-made gaps.

"We keep going."

Releasing her hand, he took the left slide while she took the right. The cement runways attached to the ground weren't too steep, but there were cracks with roots and grass jutting out, making traversing them while running a tricky maneuver. The slant shifted by varying degrees before dumping into a large basin.

At the slide's edge, Tessa stopped short and grimaced at the ankle-deep water that hid any number of allergens.

Footsteps pounded far above, and he saw James motion to someone out of sight.

She lowered herself to a seated position.

"Try to keep that wound covered," he advised, wriggling down into the basin and hurrying to her.

Curving an arm around her waist, he assisted her down and glanced at her shirt. He didn't mention the fresh blood matting the material to her skin. They'd have to deal with it later.

Their mad dash toward the concrete steps made water splash up. Tiny droplets sprayed over his arms and legs. His peripheral vision picked up movement to their right, and he saw a bald, muscular suit-clad guard advancing from the cluster of food huts and metal tables.

Mason searched for proper cover and decided on the bathroom structure a few yards from the concrete steps. With a hand on her back, he put himself between Baldy and Tessa, urging her up the stairs and across the expanse. When he saw the guard prepare to shoot, he got off a shot first. It went wide, but the guy interrupted his pursuit to duck behind a table.

Once they reached the breezeway, he felt somewhat better. They again had to dodge debris, this time tiles that had been ripped out of the ceiling. Someone had sprayed graffiti on the lockers, and broken bottles and metal cans littered the ground.

On the other side of the breezeway, they realized they were hemmed in. Thick black bars, part of the original structure, had been installed to link the bathroom building with the child's pool area. Probably to contain the children so parents didn't have to worry about them wandering off. His midsection aching, Mason gazed at the enclosure.

"Over there." Tessa indicated an area of collapsed fence.

To reach it, they'd have to wade through knee-high water and duck under bridges linking four domed play structures.

"We're going to be hooked up to antibiotic IVs after this," she sighed, forging ahead.

Their rushed progression disturbed the algae and stirred up broken bits of bark and leaves. Mason held his Glock high above the water. It was their only defense, and he couldn't let the ammo get wet. Halfway through the pool, they were shot at again.

Tessa lurched through the water and ducked behind the nearest play structure. Mason wasn't far behind. Putting her between the structure and his body, he scanned the periphery. The direction of the shot suggested it was Baldy. The breezeway was visible from their vantage point, and it was empty.

Where was James? Were there others descending upon them?

He and Tessa were both battling fatigue. She was injured, and his lungs hadn't fully recovered from the smoke. Law enforcement would investigate the areas immediately surrounding their last communication, but this was a large county. No telling how long it would take authorities to respond to their distress call.

One thing was certain—they had to keep moving.

"Let's get out of this area," he said. "Go to that next structure while I cover you."

"You'll be right behind me?"

"Yes."

She pursed her lips and blew out a breath. "All right. Here I go."

Tessa lunged through the water, and no responding shot came. Mason waited until she had reached safety to follow her. The goon shot at him. The bullet pinged off the bridge inches above his head.

She seized his arm and pulled him out of sight.

A gurgle of distress left her lips just as James appeared in the breezeway. Mason put his hand on her back. "Go!"

James raised his weapon. Mason discharged his first and managed to clip the guy.

Tessa hauled herself onto the grimy ledge and called to him. He was the target of another spray of bullets from

Baldy's direction. When he got close, she grabbed his forearm and gave him a boost up. Water sluiced from his pants and shoes. From this vantage point, he finally spotted the building he'd been looking for.

As they climbed through the gap, he explained that they would try to get to the indoor pool. They could better defend themselves there while they awaited backup.

Taking her hand, he led the way through the underbrush. Scarred, uneven pavement stood between them and the dull gray gym-like building. The exterior was pitted and crumbling, and more than half of the high windows had been punched out. The side-entrance door hung on its hinges. They would enter there.

"Ready to run?"

She nodded somberly.

He touched her cheek, distracted by her soft skin. "I want you to fix your eyes on that building. Don't look back, and don't worry about me."

"Not worry about you? Impossible."

Mason was overtaken with the urge to kiss her. *Not the right time. Not the right move.*

"Now!"

They took off, sprinting as fast as their legs could carry them. He heard the shots, felt one whiz past his ear. Mason was convinced they didn't want to kill them yet, but only wanted to wound them in order to capture them for Dante's demented purposes. Not exactly a comforting prospect. Although, he wasn't sure how committed they were to capturing them at this point. He and Tessa had evaded them for days. They were down one man, and now Bruno and James had sustained wounds.

Tessa stumbled. He caught her arm and prevented her from falling. Ahead, the gloomy interior beckoned. What would they find inside?

As they ducked under the heavy door, he heard James and his cohort shouting to each other. Tessa went first. Once inside, he hefted the door and propped it into an upright position. Because a thick layer of clouds hid the sun, there was little light coming through the high windows.

Tessa paced a few yards away. "How long until the police get here?"

"Hopefully not long." He was short on ammo, outgunned and outmanned. Their enemy had the advantage.

Mason strode the length of the cement wall. He had to check the main entrance—

A cascade of rocks striking the pool floor coincided with Tessa's scream, followed by a thud. One second, she was standing nearby, the next, she'd disappeared.

"Tessa!"

He ran to the edge of the giant pool, careful to avoid the section that had given way under her weight. She was lying on the bottom, cement chunks and tile shards in a haphazard pattern around her. Her eyes were closed, and she wasn't moving.

The fall had jarred every bone in her body. Her left ankle seemed to be the only serious injury, and she was certain it was only a sprain.

"Tessa?"

Opening her eyes, she saw Mason sprawled on his stomach and gripping the rounded ledge.

"I'm okay. I may have sprained my ankle, that's all."

His relief was temporary. "The ladders are missing, and there aren't steps for you to climb out on. Can you stand up and come over here?" He sat up and removed his belt. "I'll try and pull you out."

Tessa gingerly got to her feet and couldn't contain the hiss that escaped once she put weight on her ankle.

This was seriously going to slow them down. One positive? The new injury distracted her from the pain in her chest. She was beginning to think there was something lodged in her wound, probably glass that would have to be removed by a medical professional.

Hobbling over to the pool wall and looking up, she realized how far the distance was between her and Mason. She surveyed the rest of the basin. Although cloaked in milky shadows, she could tell the pool was all the same depth. Diving platforms were spaced out across the far side.

"Grab the belt." Mason had gotten into a crouched position and was bracing his weight against that rounded lip that had crumbled like sawdust under her. Would this section hold?

Tessa wrapped the belt around one wrist and got a secure grip with her other hand. She tried not to think about the men outside and how any minute they were going to breach the building.

Mason began to hoist her up. Almost immediately, the lip where his tennis shoe was braced disintegrated. A large chunk barely missed her cheekbone, and she let go.

"It's not going to work," she said.

The tension on the belt eased, and he lowered her to the ground so she could free her wrist.

He glanced at the broken door they'd entered through. "I'm going to walk around the pool and try and find another way out."

Tessa's gaze followed his progress, her trepidation intensifying the farther away he got.

"Got something."

He bent to pick up whatever it was he'd found, and he didn't see the far door swing open. Tessa called out a warning. Before he could react, James struck him over the head.

Mason slumped to the ground.

She willed him to get up, to speak, to do *something*.

Footsteps registered behind her, and she got a whiff of citrusy cologne that made her gag. She lifted her gaze and felt what little courage she'd had shrivel like a grape in the sun.

His smile was as cruel as ever, the promise of retribution in his black eyes striking fresh terror inside her.

He crouched at the pool's edge. "Hello, Tessa."

FIFTEEN

Those who didn't know Dante wouldn't guess from his appearance that he was a monster. Tall and physically fit, he had the face of a model and the bearing of one born into power and prestige. He wore his black hair slicked off his forehead in a wave, highlighting his patrician features and full, sculpted mouth that could so effortlessly twist with cruelty. The scar above his eyebrow—sustained during a knife fight when he was a teen—gave him just enough mystery to draw in others, who would be unaware that he was the deadly spider and they were the prey caught in his web.

"You've caused me no end of trouble, little sister," he stated calmly. "You will have to pay for that."

He called to his goons. "Get her out."

James and the other man brought over a silver ladder that looked as if it used to be attached to the cement. Together, they held it in position so that she could climb up. With no other choice, Tessa slowly ascended the unstable rungs, trying not to put weight on her injured ankle.

At the top, James clamped onto her arm and shoved her toward Dante. He caught her wrists, stopping her before she slammed into his chest. His razor-like gaze scraped over her.

"The years have not been kind to you."

His nearness made her skin crawl. "You should've stayed in New Jersey. I'm not a threat to you."

"You made yourself a target when you sided with a cop and sought to incriminate us." He smirked. "I'm sure you're aware that I don't let betrayal go unpunished, not even when it originates in my own family." With a sound of disgust, he pushed her away from him. She stumbled into the wall. "Bring Sergeant Reed to the vehicle."

"Please, Dante, leave him out of this. Mason isn't important to the family."

"Not important?" His brows winged up. "Sergeant Reed is the father of the first Vitale grandchild. That makes him very important." Gripping her chin in a bruising hold, he said with a touch of temper, "It was really bad of you, Tessa, to keep Lily's existence a secret. Father was devastated when he learned of your duplicity. I'm going to make it up to him, though. I'm going to take her to him."

Tessa couldn't speak. Her worst nightmare was coming true.

James and the other man trundled past them, dragging an unconscious Mason out of the building. Dante waved his arm with an exaggerated royal flourish to indicate she should walk ahead of him. Outside, she wasn't met with the reassuring whir of sirens or the sudden arrival of the authorities. During the too-brief trek to Dante's vehicle, she kept hoping and praying for a rescue that didn't come.

The men stowed Mason in the trunk, securing his wrists and feet with thick rope. Dante pushed Tessa into the back seat and slammed the door. He stalked around the vehicle and slid into the vacant space beside her. The trunk lid closed with a thud. She knotted her hands together and pressed them against her stomach. In his unconscious state, Mason was unable to defend himself. He could have a concussion or worse.

James got into the passenger seat and the bald one got behind the wheel. As they bumped over the neglected road, Tessa prayed they'd encounter the police. But the dilapidated buildings and half-hidden billboard came into view and, beyond them, the main road. The vehicle headed left, in the direction of Serenity, but they soon turned off onto a secondary road.

The deeper into the cove they drove, the harder her heart thumped against her rib cage.

"Is Father aware of your reasons for being here?"

"He knows I'm on a mission to collect the evidence you have on Officer Fisk's death and that I'm here to retrieve his granddaughter."

"I don't have any evidence. I told you that in the beginning."

"I don't believe you." He fiddled with his diamond cuff links. "Sergeant Reed will provide the incentive you need to talk."

"You're not planning on leaving either of us alive." The certainty chilled her to the bone. "What will Father do once he learns the truth?"

"You turned against us. Why should he care? You know, you could have had an unparalleled life, yet you threw it all away."

"I didn't want that life!" she blurted. "I never wanted it. If you hadn't forced me to return home, if you'd let me live my own life, none of this would've happened."

His expression turned vicious, and he wrapped his fingers around her throat, applying enough pressure to stop air from entering.

"Are you suggesting *I* am to blame for your treachery?"

She clawed at his fingers. Her vision turned black as her lungs stretched to a bursting point.

His phone chirped. With his free hand, he checked the caller's identity. "Saved by the business you despise," he drawled, releasing her to answer the call.

"Jack, this had better be important."

Tessa sucked in air and huddled against the door, as far away from Dante as she could possibly get. The window was cool and smooth against her hot skin. She wanted to close her eyes and give in to her misery, but she had to stay alert and remember the route they were taking. She couldn't give up hope. She had to fight to stay alive... for Lily.

As the tires ate up the miles, they left civilization behind and entered what could be part of the national park it was so wooded and isolated.

Dante ended his call and she stiffened, expecting him to pick up where he'd left off. Instead, he ignored her, his long, elegant fingers tapping his knee.

The car began to slow. A bright spot of color in the green-and-brown vista drew her gaze. The older, red-brick home was well maintained, with ivy creeping up the walls and wide, welcoming windows. The mailbox had the name *Johnson* printed on the side.

"Where are the owners?"

The driver parked the car and opened her door. She got out, and when Dante unfolded his frame on the other side, he smirked at her across the roof. Sunlight broke through the clouds behind him, shining on his hair and throwing his eyes in relief.

"Out of town."

Tessa trailed the men to the rear of the car and gulped down a moan when she saw Mason's unmoving form. He looked to be simply asleep. When they removed him from the trunk, she saw a thread of blood between his hair and shirt collar. She hated the feeling of helplessness that engulfed her mind, body and soul.

Would they die here today?

The inside of the house was clean and homey. Before she could look around for anything that might serve as a makeshift weapon, they marched her down the stairs and into a basement. This unfinished space was nothing like the first floor. Half the walls were made of dirt, and the others were cement block. There wasn't a single window. A sparkling front-load washer and dryer were out of place, as were the cabinets fitted with brightly colored fabric-organizer boxes.

James lowered Mason to the ground. He groaned, but his eyes remained shut. They propped him up against a foundation pole and wrapped thick rope around his shoulders to secure him. His head was bowed, his upper body held upright by the rope.

When they turned to her, she took a step back, only to encounter her brother's chest.

He guided her to the other pole and ordered James to bind her to it. As the rope wound around her upper body, she appealed to Dante one last time.

"Please, leave Mason out of this. I'll go home with you. I'll do whatever you say, I promise. Just don't hurt him."

He sniffed, as if she was emitting a foul stench. "You're of no worth to us any longer, Tessa."

Mason's head felt too heavy for his body. His vision, when he first opened his eyes, was blurry. When it cleared, he got a nasty dose of reality. They were at the Mafia prince's mercy. Not a good place to be. But they were alive, and he was intent on keeping them that way.

Tessa was close enough that their feet almost touched. Above her shoe, the flesh was pink and swollen. The blood on her shirt was dark, the torn material matted to her body, hinting that the wound had crusted over. When Mason's gaze landed on the fresh welts on her neck, fury funneled through him. He strained at the ropes, struggled to free his wrists and ankles.

Crouched beside her, Dante twisted toward Mason. "Ah, Sergeant Reed, you're awake. Welcome to the reunion."

"Get away from her."

Dante laughed, and the other men in the room joined in. Tessa's gaze begged him not to bring their wrath down on him. He closed his eyes and tried to calm the raging beast inside. What had he learned early on in his training? Out-of-control emotion would get him, his fellow officers and innocent civilians killed.

"I'm glad you're awake. I was about to outline my plans for Lily."

Mason's eyes snapped open.

Dante's self-satisfied air grated. "Once I'm done with you two, I'm going to take Lily home with me. I will raise her as if she were my own daughter." Ignoring Tessa's squeak of protest, he said, "I'll make sure she doesn't turn out like her mother—ungrateful and small-minded. No, Lily will be more like her Aunt Francesca, who understands the value of the Vitale legacy. Who knows? One day I may marry her to a business associate. Unlike her mother, she will do what's best for the family."

"You won't be able to get to her," Mason informed him. "My unit will guard her with their lives."

His expression turned mocking. "I captured you and Tessa in a matter of days. I'll have Lily before the week is out. Once I do, I'll make sure she forgets you both.

Day by day, week by week, year by year, I'll erase her memories of you."

Mason made the mistake of looking at Tessa. Tears streamed unchecked down her cheeks, and he felt them like rivers of burning acid over his heart.

God, I can't fail her. I can't fail our daughter. Please don't let evil win.

Dante angled back to Tessa. "Sister dearest, it's time for you to give me the information I seek. You recorded that long-ago conversation with Father. You know, the one that incriminated us for planning Officer Fisk's death? Where is it? On a flash drive? Laptop?"

Her lips trembled. "There is no recording, Dante. Not in my possession. Fisk was listening in with his equipment. I was supposed to get the confession while he did the rest. You burst in before Father admitted his guilt."

The skin around his eyes tightened, and the veins at his temples bulged. He lifted a hand in a silent signal. Tessa's eyes widened as James stalked across the room and stood over Mason. He'd removed his dress shirt, but had been wearing a white cotton shirt underneath. His partner had stitched him up where Mason had clipped him.

James balled his fingers into an impressive fist, hauled back and slammed it into Mason's face. Fire exploded in his cheek, and the force of the blow whipped his head to the left. His existing headache grew by leaps and bounds, but he forgot it when James's boot connected with his ribs. Once. Twice. Three times. Mason felt the instant the bone gave under pressure.

Tessa's pleas bordered on hysteria. He'd give anything to remove her from this equation, to spare her from her brother's callous disregard for human life.

"Stop, Dante! You have to believe me. There is no evidence to be found! Didn't you check Fisk's belongings?"

He heard her gasp. Mason lifted his head. Dante's hand cupped her throat, poised to cut off her air supply.

"Do you remember when I made you watch Skinny Walter's murder?"

Her hands fisted on the cold cement. She swallowed convulsively.

"I will make you watch Sergeant Reed's death if you don't tell me. It won't be merciful, I promise you."

"Boss, Bruno's upstairs," James interrupted. "He's got the food you asked for."

Dante ignored him. "Tessa, I had one of my men search your place in Georgia. He didn't find anything, which leads me to believe you brought it with you. When I finish my meal, I expect you to have a different answer. Understand?"

At her nod, he finally removed his hand and stood. He left the basement, closing the door at the top of the stairs and locking them in.

SIXTEEN

"Oh, Mason…" Tessa's voice was thick with sorrow and regret. "If I could change the past—"

"You're not to blame for his actions. Frankly, how you managed to escape his clutches in the first place is a mystery." He shifted to get a better look around, unable to mask the pain vibrating through his midsection. As long as his busted rib hadn't punctured a lung, he'd be okay. "We have to find a way out of here."

"How? There's no window. No weapons that I can see. Neither of us have a phone." She rested her hands on her lap, and her brow furrowed. "Hold on."

Tessa dug into her pants pocket and fished out a small silver object.

"Why do you have nail clippers in your pocket?"

She turned the clippers this way and that. "I trimmed Lily's fingernails this morning…" Her eyes widened, and she began to clip at the thick rope holding her fast to the pole. "If I can get free, I can untie you."

"We might have a chance." A slim one, but he wasn't going to discourage her.

Mason understood that if they did succeed, it would be God's will that they do so. He understood what Daniel must've felt in the lion's den, what Shadrach, Meshach and Abednego had felt entering that fiery furnace. Death was almost certain. Yet, God had other plans. Even though his and Tessa's situation seemed impossible, He had the power and authority to make a way of rescue.

The boards creaked overhead as the men walked around. Occasionally, laughter would interrupt their conversation. How they could enjoy a meal, as if they weren't about to commit murder, was beyond him. In his line of work, he'd encountered plenty of selfish, angry people who committed crimes for various reasons. Many of them had become slaves to drugs and alcohol, and addiction drove their actions. He hadn't come across any that killed for sport. Unfortunately, Dante appeared to enjoy hurting others, and he paid his henchmen to do his bidding.

Watching Tessa chip away at those ropes, he realized the self-righteous anger he'd been nurturing since she'd returned was gone. The bitterness was gone. The past couldn't be changed, his part or her part. Without those emotions to fuel his reactions, he was left with feelings for Tessa that had survived the breakup, feelings he couldn't let overrule caution and sound judgment.

"Got one." Tessa strained against the remaining strands. When they didn't budge, she started in on another one.

Mason silently cheered her on while reexamining their surroundings. There wasn't much that he could see that would help them fight their way out.

The minutes it took for her to free herself felt like days. He listened to the activity upstairs, trying to gauge how long they would linger over the meal. He didn't want to imagine Dante's reaction if he caught them in the middle of an escape attempt.

Tessa gave a small cry of triumph when she wriggled

free. Hurrying over, she worked on untying his wrists. It took longer than it should have.

"My hands are sweaty," she lamented, trying again to undo the knot.

"You're doing fine."

Finally, she succeeded. He instructed her to work on the knots tying him to the pole while he freed his ankles. The awkward angle exacerbated his rib pain. He gritted his teeth and worked faster. A chair slid across the floorboards in the room above them, and he wondered if that signaled their meal was over.

The knob jiggled. He and Tessa both froze. Someone called out, and footsteps moved away from the stairs. Her fingers flew into a frenzy. He felt the rope give way.

Moving around to his side, Tessa placed an arm around him and helped him to stand. His head felt too light for his body, and the room listed to the right.

"Mason?" she whispered, pressing close against him.

"I'm fine."

Opening his eyes, he managed a tight smile. "We need a weapon."

They quickly searched the space around the laundry organizer unit. Tessa motioned for him to follow her beneath the stairs. On the other side, there were numerous shelves that held jars of homemade jams and soups. In the corner, he located a broom. He whacked it against his knee, and the wooden handle snapped into two pieces.

"Mason, look." Standing at a point by the middle of the cement wall, Tessa went on her tiptoes and tugged on a swath of thick fabric. As it fell away, a ground-level well-type window was revealed. That window evoked the first smile he'd seen on her face in ages.

Excited now, she retrieved a metal bucket from the

corner, then turned it over, climbed up and shoved at the window. At first, it didn't budge.

"Is it unlocked?"

"Yes. It's just stuck." Tessa wouldn't give up. Nor would she let him help. The window began to open, inch by inch.

Sweat dampened the back of his neck. Would the men hear the occasional squeaks and investigate? As soon as the thought entered his mind, the upstairs door opened and closed. Someone began to descend into the basement.

Tessa whirled around and nearly toppled off the bucket. Mason put his finger to his lips. Wielding one half of the broken broom handle at chest level and gripping the other at his waist, he crept over to the stairs. Baldy got to the bottom and, noticing they weren't where he'd left them, turned to alert the others. It was the opening Mason needed.

He jabbed the handle into the man's stomach, knocking him back several steps. He used the second piece to whack his temple area with all the force he could muster. Baldy crumpled to the ground, unconscious but alive. Mason relieved him of his phone and weapon.

At his urging, Tessa climbed out first. He wriggled through and joined her on solid ground. Every breath delivered stabbing pain that radiated through his upper body. His head throbbed, making it difficult to concentrate.

She folded her hand into his and gazed at him with those beautiful hazel eyes—she was looking to him for direction. Tessa trusted him with her life.

He swiftly evaluated their surroundings. "We'll stay with the tree line," he said, pointing to the natural property border that curved around to the only road access. Once they had reached the relative safety of the woods, he said, "Did you see other homes during the ride in? Do you remember how far we are from the main road?"

"Several miles." She frowned at him, concern and doubt written on her face. "This house is the last on this road. The owners must like their privacy."

He squeezed her hand and released it. He fished the goon's phone from his pocket. "Password protected. No surprise there. I can't make a personal call, but I'm going to try to reach the authorities."

He hit the emergency link and dialed 911. They continued walking while he spoke to the dispatcher. Tessa's limp became more pronounced, and he shortened his strides.

Distant shouting announced their absence had been discovered. Tessa seized his arm, and he informed the 911 operator that he would have to put him on mute. At the sound of an approaching car, they crouched behind some underbrush. Mason removed Baldy's revolver from his waistband.

Through a slender gap in the plants, he saw the sedan cruising at maybe five miles per hour. All the windows were rolled down, and Dante, Bruno and James were scouring both sides of the road, guns glinting in the sun. Baldy was slumped in the back seat, his eyes closed.

Tessa uttered faint snatches of a prayer.

The car jolted to a stop not far from their hiding place. And then the sirens echoed off the peaks above and through the cove. The timing couldn't have been more perfect. Dante ordered James to drive.

Neither Mason nor Tessa dared breathe as the sedan disappeared from sight. The minutes ticked by. The sirens grew louder.

"Are they really gone?" She twisted toward him, hopeful yet wary.

Mason put away the weapon, then slowly got to his feet and inched to the road's edge. "They're really gone."

With a joyful exclamation, she limped over to where he stood and threw her arms around his neck. Mason wrapped his arm around her lower back and buried his face in the curve of her shoulder.

The enormity of their close call threatened to overwhelm him. He'd been shot at before, by pumped-up drug users and petty thieves determined to avoid jail time. This encounter with Dante was on a different level. This was personal, and the man was cruel. No matter what, Mason had to prevent him from getting to Tessa again.

Mason lifted his head. She'd grown more beautiful during their time apart and, right now, there was no fear, no guilt, no wishing for a do-over. She was looking at him like she used to, like he filled her life with joy and meaning. He'd forgotten how easily she could make him feel like a superhero.

He carefully placed his hands on either side of her face, and then he kissed her full on the lips. Gently, sweetly, shyly. She leaned into him, and his ribs spasmed.

Mason pulled away as the first cruiser approached. After placing the gun on the ground, he held up his hands. He recognized the officer behind the wheel—Officer Jolene Hammond. She was quickly joined by two others. After getting the details, she stayed with them while the others pursued Dante. He borrowed her phone to call Silver. His friend had been trying to contact him and was audibly relieved to hear they were safe. Silver reassured him that Lily was as happy as a lark because Gia was catering to her every whim. The statement made Mason smile. His mom was born to be a grandmother.

An ambulance arrived and whisked them both to the hospital. Tessa was subdued during transport, and he couldn't get a read on her. Was she overcome with fatigue? Shock? Or was it the kiss?

When they were alone, Mason would have to tell her nothing had changed. The moment of tenderness had been the result of intense gratitude that they'd escaped Dante's clutches. He didn't regret the kiss—it had been a healing balm after a harrowing day. He did regret any confusion his actions had caused her. He didn't know what she envisioned for her future, didn't know how she felt about him. One thing was for certain—friendship was the best they could hope for.

SEVENTEEN

Tessa counted the ceiling tiles to keep from drifting off. She couldn't close her eyes. If she did, she'd see Dante's sneering face again. She'd relive the terror of watching his goon hurt Mason.

There was a knock on the tiny corner room the ER staff had stuck her in. The security guard posted outside announced the visitor and waited for Tessa's assent to admit her.

"Candace."

The blonde strode inside, closed the door and hung a nondescript backpack on the doorknob. Her face was a study in concern. "I brought you a change of clothes."

"Have you seen Mason?" Tessa scooted upright. "How is he?"

She perched on the lone chair and propped her purse on her knees. "I was with him just now. The doctor wants to keep him for one night, not only because of his head injury and busted ribs, but because of his recent smoke inhalation. As you might've guessed, my brother is insisting he will recuperate faster at home." Her shadowed gaze held Tessa's. "How are you?"

Her fingers skimmed the bandage poking out from the hospital gown. "Happy they got the glass out of my wound relatively quickly. It needed a couple of stitches." She gestured to the foot of the bed. "My ankle is merely sprained."

"He told me what happened. I'd be a puddle on the floor right now. You're a strong woman."

"I'm a mess. I'd be a bigger mess if not for my faith." God was her protector, her strength, her everything.

"It's interesting that you and Mason both embarked on your faith journeys after your relationship imploded."

"God used our hurt and disappointment to draw us to Him."

She cocked her head to one side. "Do you think there's a chance for reconciliation? You still care about each other. Don't try to convince me otherwise."

Tessa's cheeks heated as she recalled Mason's kiss. It had been the best of kisses and the worst of kisses. She'd sensed his iron-clad restraint as he held back four years' worth of emotion. For her, that kiss hadn't settled anything. It had spawned questions she was afraid to get answers to.

"I can't answer that right now."

Candace smiled. "That's not an outright no."

"You wouldn't mind if Mason and I…?" She couldn't put voice to her words. A second chance with Mason? Tessa hadn't let herself entertain the possibility. Even now, she was afraid to hope.

"Do I have reservations? Not as many now that I know everything that transpired between you. My brother was the happiest he's ever been when he was with you. These past years, he's been going through the motions. Not professionally—his career challenges him and gives him great satisfaction. His personal life is another story. He's never gotten over you, Tessa. And now, you share this amazing little girl. Surely you could work things out."

"You're excited to be an aunt, aren't you?"

"I admit I have a personal stake. If you and Mason are together, I get more time with my niece."

Tessa felt her mouth stretch into a smile. "I've missed our friendship, Candace. Do you think we could start over?"

"I'd like that."

The nurse arrived and gave Tessa instructions on wound care. Before she had a chance to change, Mason showed up in a wheelchair. The right side of his face was battered and bruised.

"Are you ready to go see Lily?"

His slight smile and easy tone couldn't distract her from his careful, solemn demeanor. Was that due to his physical discomfort? The weight of their shared trauma? Or regret that he'd kissed her?

"Shouldn't you stay the night?" she asked.

"No, I shouldn't. My ribs are cracked, not broken. My internal organs are fine."

"What about your head? You lost consciousness for quite a while. Do you have a concussion?"

"Tessa, I'll rest easier at the cabin. Rest equals faster recuperation."

"Have you heard from the Pigeon Forge PD?"

"Dante got away." His nostrils flared. "We're going to blast these guys' faces across social media and air them on the local news. Silver even mentioned paying for a billboard. By tomorrow, the tips will be pouring in."

Tips took time to sort through, however. And Serenity's law-enforcement entities were stretched thin. This was the beginning of the tourist season, and Tessa's predicament couldn't be their sole focus.

Pigeon Forge PD escorted them from the hospital to the mounted-police truck parked at the abandoned water park. Candace had driven her own vehicle to the hospital, which left Tessa to drive the truck. Her injuries weren't as severe as Mason's, and she hadn't been given pain medication. One of the officers volunteered to continue with them the rest of the way, and they gladly accepted.

At the cabin, Silver and Cruz's welcome was grim. That Silver couldn't find anything to joke about was telling. His eyes smoldered violet fire as he took in Mason's battered face and the bruises on her neck.

Lily heard the commotion at the door and streaked through the living room like a comet. "Mommy!"

Tessa hoisted her into her arms and reveled in the sweet show of affection. *Thank You, Lord Jesus, for bringing us back to her.*

"Guess what? Mimi and me made lots and lots of cookies!" Lily played with Tessa's curls. "And we made castles out of Play-Doh and watched shows."

Mimi? Her gaze found Gia, who was traversing the spacious living area as she wiped her hands on a kitchen towel. "I hope that's okay. I didn't explain any details."

"It's fine. Thank you for entertaining her all day."

"It was my pleasure." Tessa shifted, and Gia got a full glimpse of Mason. She gasped.

"Mom, I'm fine," he inserted, moving forward to kiss her cheek. The climb up the steep porch stairs had taken its toll. He was in pain and trying to hide it.

"After we heard about the 911 call and the loss of contact, I prayed for you both nonstop."

Lily leaned sideways in her arms and reached for Mason. He smiled and would have taken her weight, but Tessa shifted away. "Not a good idea. Let's sit on the couch."

When they were settled, Lily climbed onto his lap and touched his face. "You have a boo-boo."

He took hold of her fingers and pressed a kiss to them. "It will heal. Have you had many boo-boos?"

"No." She shook her head. "Mommy doesn't let me climb up the slide. She makes me slide down like I'm 'posed to."

He chuckled, then grimaced. "Your mom is one smart lady."

"Will you build a Play-Doh stable with me?"

"That's a great idea. First, I have to wash up, and then your mom and I need to eat something."

Gia gestured behind her. "I assembled lasagna earlier. I'll put it in the oven to bake. Lily can help me with the salad if she'd like."

Lily scrambled off Mason's lap. Candace entered the cabin and intercepted her.

"Where are you going so fast?"

"Cooking with Mimi."

Candace's eyebrows were swallowed by her bangs. "Mimi, huh? Do you mind if I help?"

Lily nodded and grabbed her hand. Together, they went to wash up and gather the vegetables.

Mason lightly touched Tessa's hand. "We need to tell her the truth as soon as possible, before my mom and sister do it for us."

"Tonight?"

He considered the idea. "Tomorrow morning after breakfast. We'll both be refreshed."

"Okay." Tessa wasn't sure how much of the conversation Lily would understand, but she was ready for her to know Mason's true role in her life.

"You and I should talk, as well."

Her stomach lurched. "I think I know what you want to discuss, and it can wait until we're no longer in danger."

He appeared to be on the verge of disagreeing. Then he thought better of it.

"I want you to know that I wouldn't dream of hurting you again."

He obviously regretted that moment in the woods. "I know, Mason. I feel the same."

"We're on the same page then."

"Yes."

Were they really? Honestly, she hadn't ever stopped loving him. If she was offered a second chance with the love of her life, she'd snatch it. But he wasn't looking to be with her again, and she couldn't blame him.

Mason tucked into the mouthwatering meal his mom had prepared, content to absorb the conversation around him. The shower had washed away the grime and loosened his muscles, and, while the medication had merely taken the edge off his discomfort, he felt well enough to sit with his family and friends and thank the Lord for his blessings.

Silver, Cruz and Raven occupied one side of the rustic table. Candace and his mom were seated at either end. Lily was in a booster seat between him and Tessa. A wrought-iron globe chandelier cast a broad circle of light over the serving bowls, dinnerware and glasses. The meaty, tomato-rich aroma melded with his mom's tangy homemade salad dressing and garlic knots. After a solemn prayer of thanks offered by Gia, everyone dug in.

Mason was pleased to see that Lily was willing to try most foods. The more time he spent with her, the more he came to appreciate Tessa's mothering skills. She'd managed to keep their daughter safe in a town where she had no roots and no family. Not only that, but she'd also given her a normal upbringing.

Over Lily's head, he studied Tessa's profile. She had also showered and changed into fresh clothes. Her glossy black hair had been tamed into a tidy French braid, and tasteful earrings sparkled at her ears. Since he'd known her, she hadn't gone for flashy or expensive. She'd grown up surrounded by luxury, but she'd turned her back on that life out of principle. That said something about her character.

She glanced up and caught him staring. For a moment, they got lost in each other, reliving that moment of rejoicing in the aftermath of ugliness. He would like to tell her she was the strongest woman he'd ever met. He would like to ask her exactly where she'd gotten the courage to defy the mighty Vitale family.

The invisible connection was broken when Lily tugged on Tessa's sleeve and asked for more juice. He looked away, only to encounter the combined focus of Silver and Cruz. Their disquiet was obvious. Silver, especially, had reason to worry. He'd had a front-row seat to Mason's implosion following Tessa's departure.

He gave a brief shake of his head, a silent signal that he was fine.

After the meal, Tessa and Candace whisked Lily to the master bath for her bedtime routine and his unit cornered him outside on the balcony. Cruz propped his body against the corner post while Silver paced. Raven dropped into the chair beside him.

Light from the dining room combated the hazy, purple-tinged dusk cloaking the woods on either side of the cabin. The mountain peaks in the distance had become smudged, indistinct shapes.

"What happened out there?" Silver said. "I want a bullet-point list."

Fingers of fatigue whispered over him. This day

ranked up there as the second worst of his life, and he wasn't eager to explain the gory details. But his partners were putting their lives on the line for him, Tessa and Lily, and they deserved to know exactly what sort of enemy they were dealing with.

He inhaled a lungful of honeysuckle air, trying to ignore the unhappy response in his rib cage. The others were quiet as he relayed the facts with as much professional detachment as he could muster. They didn't immediately respond. Their silence added an ominous weight to the otherwise innocent night.

Cruz crossed and uncrossed his ankles. "I've come across his type before, back in Texas. Our department lost three officers before we managed to capture the guy."

Silver ground his teeth. "We're not losing anyone. I've reached out to a private security firm with a stellar reputation and hired two of their men. They start in the morning."

Mason didn't have the energy to launch a proper protest. "You hired them without consulting me?"

"We need the assistance. We're spread too thin."

Mason couldn't afford private security. "It will cost a fortune."

"I'm footing the bill."

"I can't let you do that. I have a home to rebuild and a truck to replace. There's no telling how long before I could repay you."

"I don't want to be repaid."

"Foster—"

"Whoa." He halted and held up a gloved hand. "Stop with the parent-given name, will you? We can't keep going on little to no sleep, and we can't monopolize the patrol unit or the sheriff's deputies. Let me do this."

His friend shelling out loads of money for Mason's benefit wasn't fair.

"Think of Tessa," he urged. "And your daughter."

Dante's sneering face flashed into his mind. "I owe you, brother."

Their phones buzzed simultaneously. Raven got to hers first. "Social-media blitz is a go," she said. "Dante and his henchmen won't be able to buy a pack of gum without looking over their shoulders."

"I'm still waiting on my billboard contact to return my call," Silver said, scrolling through his phone. "I'd like to get their faces in a high-traffic area."

"Mayor Chesney will have something to say about that," Raven said. "Advertising the presence of Mafia criminals is bad for tourism."

"Tourists getting taken hostage and shot by said Mafia criminals is also bad for tourism," he returned with an arched brow.

"I'd like to hear you say that to the mayor's face," she said, softly laughing.

"Did the Pascals get back to Florida yet?" Mason asked.

"Lindsey put them personally on the plane."

The sliding glass doors swooshed open, and Lily padded out in her pajamas. She searched the semidarkness and zeroed in on him. He set aside his phone and put his hands out to frame her tiny waist, lest she decide to leap into his arms.

"You smell good enough to eat," he teased, deliberately sniffing her hair. "Is your shampoo scented with lemons?"

She giggled. "No, silly, not lemons."

"Hmm." He sniffed her sleeve. "Is it watermelon?"

"Nuh-uh." She braced her hands atop his.

He smelled her cheek. "I know. It's pancake syrup."

"No, it's apples!"

"Ah, apples. Why didn't I think of that?" He spotted Tessa, who was standing near the sliding doors and watching them with a tired smile.

"You're off to bed, huh?"

"Candace is going to read me a book."

"You'll have to tell me about it over breakfast."

"Okay." Lily surprised him with a kiss on his cheek.

His partners bade her good-night and watched as she reentered the house. Tessa offered a half wave and followed her inside.

Mason closed his eyes and asked God to grant her dreamless, restorative sleep. He didn't like to think what the hours ahead might bring. Each time he worked a tragic car accident or took part in a search-and-rescue operation that morphed into body recovery, he replayed the events in his head for days. He envisioned the victims and relived the relatives' grieving reactions. After what he and Tessa had been through, there would be flashbacks and memories that refused to budge.

"I'm going home." Raven's announcement brought him out of his private reverie. Looking down at him, she placed her hand on his shoulder. "Get some rest."

"That's my goal."

She jabbed her finger at the others. "You two, don't keep him out here much longer. He's practically falling asleep where he sits."

Cruz pushed off the post. "I'll walk you out."

"Aren't you the gallant one," she quipped, nudging his shoulder.

He looked dubious. "I've never been called anything close to that."

They entered the cabin, their banter trailing behind

them. Silver assumed Cruz's former spot and crossed his arms as he regarded Mason with a hooded gaze.

"Should I be worried?" he drawled.

"My lungs and ribs will heal."

His friend's expression didn't change. "I like Tessa. Always have. But she has the power to send you back into the abyss. I don't want to see that happen."

Mason pushed his fingers through his hair and tried not to think about that kiss. "I'm not the same man I used to be."

"Because of your faith, I know."

If they hadn't spoken about spiritual matters before, Mason would've missed the hint of challenge in Silver's voice.

Resting his hands on the chair arms, Mason said, "You can't measure God's characteristics as a Heavenly Father against your earthly one."

"Easy for you to say. You hit the dad jackpot." He fisted his gloved hands.

Mason searched for the right response. Lewis Reed had had his share of faults, like everyone else, but he'd been a hero in Mason's eyes. Following his early passing, it had taken Mason a long time to work through his grief. He still missed him. Silver hadn't been so fortunate, with either of his parents, and he bore the scars to this day. His childhood trauma stood between him and a lasting, personal relationship with God. Mason prayed that someday, Silver would lay his burdens down at Jesus's feet and find healing.

"I'm not interested in discussing my messed-up family," Silver inserted.

"I can't give you the answers you're searching for." He didn't know exactly what was happening between him and Tessa. While they hadn't discussed the kiss outright, she'd seemingly agreed with him that it hadn't been the best idea. They'd waded through enough hurt, and they were both intent on maintaining peace for their daughter's sake.

Something clicked in his mind, and he turned the tables. "Is my experience with Tessa the reason you've avoided commitment?"

A sardonic laugh burst forth. "No, what it did was cement my decision to stay single. Emotional entanglements are the last thing a guy like me needs. Besides, I would make a woman miserable long-term."

"That's a convenient lie you've told yourself, brother."

Silver's phone buzzed. He fished it from his pocket and skimmed the message. "Lindsey has a pressing question about a reservation. I have to call her."

"I'll give you some privacy."

As he trudged to his bedroom, fatigue dogging his steps, Mason wondered what the future held for Silver and if his friend would remain stubbornly alone for the rest of his life. Would he choose the safety of solitude or would he take a chance on someone?

His own future was a huge question mark, as well. The idea of Tessa settling down in Serenity and eventually marrying someone else made his chest ache and his stomach churn. As he tested the front-door lock, he glanced down the hallway toward her room. Just like in the past, he found himself wanting to spend every minute with her. An alarming prospect.

He comforted himself with the knowledge that he didn't have to make any decisions regarding the future right now. They had an enemy to overcome first.

EIGHTEEN

Tessa jerked upright, lungs heaving, as she tried to get her bearings. The night-light in the bathroom bathed the bed and dresser in a triangle of light. She wasn't in that dank basement anymore. Her pajama shirt clung to her clammy skin. Nausea roiled through her middle. Threading her curls off her face, she studied Lily's peaceful form beside her and tried to shake the vestiges of the dream.

Folding back the comforter, she slid out of bed. Her sore ankle protested, and she hobbled into the bathroom, where she splashed cold water on her face and pulled on the wrap that matched her new striped pajama shirt and pants. Wide-awake now, she slipped on her sandals, crept through the silent cabin and emerged into the night. The air carried the scents of honey and flowers' perfume. Crickets' chirrups performed a woodland symphony. Stretched out above her, sparkly diamonds patterned the canvas of black sky. God's handiwork never failed to amaze her.

"Hey."

She jerked toward the source of the greeting, her hand flying to her chest.

"Sorry. I didn't mean to startle you."

There was no mistaking Mason's voice. As her eyes

adjusted, she was able to discern his body from the shadows. He was lounging on the hand-carved bench tucked between twin planters.

Tessa circled the wrought-iron table to get to him. "You can't sleep, either?"

His legs were stretched out, ankles propped on one another, and his arm rested along the benchtop. "I got a couple of hours' worth. I was hoping you'd fare better than me."

She sat without asking permission and clasped her hands on her lap. "I had a bad dream."

Mason was quiet for long moments. "I was hoping you wouldn't. Want to talk about it?"

Her mouth went dry as she thought about what had unfolded at the water park and inside the redbrick house. "Not really."

His arm left the bench to curve around her shoulders. He moved with care, no doubt to protect his ribs from sudden movements. Or maybe he didn't want to startle her again. Either way, she liked the contact. She liked being close to him.

"I am sure of one thing," she muttered.

"Yeah? What's that?"

"I'm going to avoid basements for a while."

"Good idea." She heard the smile in his tone.

They soaked in the serene night, content to draw comfort from each other's presence. She assumed he found her closeness comforting. He kept his arm around her as if it was the most natural thing in the world. Occasionally, his fingers whispered over her shoulder, the soft caress unhurried.

Sitting there together, Tessa was hurtled into the past…to a time when they were in sync, when their lives were effortlessly entwined.

"You were amazing," he murmured. "I always knew you were strong and resourceful. I didn't know how strong until yesterday."

"I was petrified." She shuddered, remembering the beating he'd suffered. "I thought I was going to watch you die."

Mason shifted and tucked her against his side. She rested her cheek against his chest and inhaled his heady scent. The cotton fabric stretched across his muscular torso was soft against her skin. His heart pounded a reassuring rhythm. When he smoothed his hand over her unruly hair and kissed the top of her head, she closed her eyes and sighed. This was as close to perfection as she could get.

She didn't dare speak or move, lest she shatter the moment. Minutes stretched by, and she relaxed into him. The tension ebbed from her.

"I have an idea."

She opened her eyes. "Tell me."

"You need rest. I'll sit outside your room until you go to sleep."

She reluctantly lifted her head and shifted out of his half embrace. "That's a thoughtful offer. You need rest, too. More than I do, in fact."

"I want you to drift off with the assurance that you're safe, I'm safe and Lily is safe." Leaving the bench, he held out his hand. "Come on."

Not wanting him to strain his ribs, she stood on her own and then fitted her palm against his. Once inside with the door secure, he chose a cushioned chair from the entry area and scooted it down the hallway. He stationed himself across from her door and pulled out his phone.

Tessa rested her hand on the knob. "You're really sweet for doing this."

"What can I say? I'm a sweet guy."

The screen light allowed her to see his grin and shining eyes. His busted face, too. Her heart squeezed with tender fondness for this brave man. The renewed sense of solidarity between them filled her with gratitude. He might never love her again, but she had hope she'd win his good opinion and respect.

Bracing her weight against the chair, she bent and brushed a kiss on his noninjured cheek. His skin was part smooth, part prickly, advertising his need for a shave.

His forehead furrowed. "What was that for?"

"For being you." Swallowing the lump in her throat, she said her good-night.

Beneath the covers again, she fell asleep within minutes of her head touching the pillow. What seemed like a short time later, she was awoken by Lily's lilting chatter. Sunlight peeping around the curtains assured her that morning had arrived without a single bad dream.

Lily bounced on the bed. "Look, Mommy! Mason made us pancakes!"

Tessa sat up and spotted him near the room's fireplace, setting a tray on the coffee table. The aromas of rich coffee, spicy sausages and something fruity brought her fully awake. He straightened and turned, white teeth flashing in his beard-shadowed face.

"I made the good kind of pancakes," he said with a wink. "No surprises."

Lily slid off the mattress and pattered over to him. "Will you cut mine? And pour syrup?"

His smile turned protective and proud as he gazed down at her. Smoothing his hand over her curls, he nodded. "I'll work on that while your mom gets dressed."

Choosing a chair that had its back to the room, he began readying Lily's breakfast. Tessa hurried into the

bathroom and chose from her meager belongings—
another tourist-geared T-shirt, jeans and sandals. She
looked in the mirror and grimaced at her reflection. Her
skin was paler than usual, giving her freckles center
stage, and there were circles under her eyes. There was
nothing to be done about it, so she put on her shiny lip
gloss and applied curl-taming gel to her mane.

Tessa joined the others and reached for coffee. He'd
prepared a trio of plates piled high with fluffy pancakes,
sausages and strawberries. "How did you have the energy
for this? Did you get any rest at all?"

Having gotten Lily settled, he got comfortable with
his own plate in his lap. "I stayed in the hallway for about
thirty minutes, until I heard you snoring. I—"

"I do not snore."

Eyes sparkling, he forked a strawberry. "Eat your pancakes, Tess. Tell me those aren't superior to your pink—"

She cleared her throat and inclined her head toward
Lily, who was currently licking maple syrup off her fingers and absorbing every word.

He smirked. "She obviously likes them."

"Why are you in such a good mood?"

He looked over at Lily. "Because we're about to have
a momentous conversation."

"Keep her age in mind, okay? I'm not sure how much
she'll understand. I don't want you to be disappointed."

"I won't be." Anticipation buzzed through him. He'd
initially decided to wait until the danger had passed, but
yesterday had reminded him that the future wasn't guar-
anteed.

Tessa was perched on the chair behind where Lily sat
on her knees, hunkered over the coffee table. Tessa bal-

anced her breakfast on the fat cushion arm and found a safe spot for her coffee mug on the small table beside it.

She dipped a slice of sausage in the syrup and shot him a tremulous smile. "I'm happy and relieved this day has come."

Lily quickly finished her breakfast and would've shot off to watch her favorite show if Tessa hadn't called her back. "Mason has something he'd like to talk to you about."

She draped over his chair. "What is it?"

Butterflies fluttered in his chest. He set aside his plate and took her small, plump, slightly sticky hand in his. "Lily, have you ever thought you might like to have a dad?"

She bounced on her toes. "Tommy Hamilton doesn't have a dad."

From across the coffee table, Tessa clarified, "Tommy is in her library story group."

"Maggie's mom went to heaven," Lily said, her eyes big.

"Is Maggie also in your story group?"

"She's at church."

"I see. Well, your mom and I are old friends…" He paused to collect his thoughts and decided to just come out with it. "Lily, you don't have to call me 'Mason' anymore. I'm your dad."

She ceased bouncing and blinked up at him. "You are?"

His heart swelled with the drive to protect this tiny human. "Yes, ladybug, I am."

"Will you make me yellow pancakes every morning?"

He chuckled. Before Tessa ducked her head to hide a smile, he saw that her eyes were suspiciously bright.

"Not every morning, but as often as I can."

"Will me and Mommy live with you?"

He licked his lips. "Do you remember that there was a fire at my house?"

"Uh-huh. It's broken."

"That's right. My house has to be fixed. After that, you will stay with me a lot."

"But what about Mommy?"

Mason avoided looking Tessa's way. Did she feel as sad about managing two separate households, with Lily bouncing between, as he did? "Well, we'll have to figure that out. As soon as we do, we'll let you know."

"Can I watch my show now?"

"Not with those dirty hands," Tessa said, standing. "I'll help you get the syrup off."

While they were in the bathroom, he sipped his coffee. Lily's response hadn't been as jubilant as he'd expected, but he reminded himself she was only three.

There was a knock on the door, and Silver poked his head in. "We've had a sighting."

Mason abandoned his coffee and went into the hallway. "Where?"

"We got a call from a concerned citizen in the Bear Ridge neighborhood about an hour ago. I'm meeting Lieutenant Polk and a couple of patrol officers. I'll report in as soon as I know something." His violet gaze shifted behind Mason, to the remnants of their breakfast. "How did it go with Lily?"

"Good. She didn't pose as many tough questions as I thought she might." He hooked his thumb toward the bathroom. "Give me a moment to tell Tessa I'm leaving."

"You're not going."

Silver was his best friend, which gave him the right to express his opinion. But Mason outranked him. Before he could speak, his friend cut him off.

"In this situation and with your injuries, you'd be a distraction, not an asset."

Mason didn't like what he was hearing.

"You know I'm right," Silver persisted. "Put yourself in Tessa's shoes. After everything that happened yesterday, is she going to be comfortable alone with my newly hired private security guards standing over her?"

"Fine, I'll sit this one out. I expect regular updates."

"You got it."

He relayed the development to Tessa when she and Lily emerged. Her tension abated somewhat when he told her he was staying. Silver had made the right call, after all.

"Are you up for a shopping trip?"

She had gone to clear her and Lily's plates from the coffee table. Instead, she straightened and stared at him. "Shopping? Now?"

"We'll stay local. There's a shop in the square that has everything you and Lily need to replenish what you lost in the fire."

"Are there toys?" Lily asked, her eyes alight with excitement.

He bent to her level and chucked her chin. "If that shop doesn't have toys, we'll search until we find some."

She clapped her hands together. Tessa was still uncertain, gauging by her expression.

"We'll have professional bodyguards with us the entire time. I'll be armed, as well."

"We are running low on toothpaste and other toiletries."

"This excursion is for clothes and shoes. You might even find the slipper-style you like so well."

"Ballet flats," she corrected, grinning.

"Yeah, those things."

As soon as the breakfast dishes were cleaned and put away, they got acquainted with Silver's hired guards, Tyson and Angus, and were soon driving down the mountain to the heart of Serenity.

Lily radiated excitement. She'd been mostly confined indoors since their arrival. The promise of a new toy was also at the forefront of her mind.

The square was usually bustling on beautiful spring days, and this morning was no exception. Mason waited for a parking spot to open directly in front of the Mint Julep Boutique. Tyson and Angus scored one nearby a few minutes later. Once the men were stationed out front, Mason ushered Tessa and Lily inside the feminine, colorful shop. He greeted the owner, Sally Decker, and took great pleasure in introducing Lily as his daughter. Sally didn't attempt to hide her surprise, and he knew the word would spread through Serenity like wildfire. He didn't mind. It would save him from repeated explanations. He took Lily to the toy-and-book area to allow Tessa time to peruse the clothing.

Lily's mission seemed to be to handle every single stuffed animal and book in stock. This was Mason's first shopping excursion with a toddler, and he found her enthusiasm charming, though it was no small task to replace everything just so. He made sure to face the shop door and windows, occasionally checking on the hired bodyguards. Silver had vouched for their professionalism, and Mason trusted his friend's instincts.

"I want this one." Lily clutched a white-and-pink unicorn to her chest and looked at him with pleading big brown eyes. "This one, too." She snagged a board book from the shelf. He was certain that with time and experience, he'd learn to say no to her. For now, he couldn't help but succumb.

"What do you say, Lily?" Tessa interjected. Several items of clothing were draped over her arms, and a pair of child-sized sandals dangled from her fingers.

"Please, Daddy?"

His gaze jerked back to Lily's round face, his heart skipping with joy over one simple word. "Yes, you may have those two things. Let's go pay."

He and Tessa wrangled over who should foot the bill. In the end, she acquiesced, probably because other patrons had entered the shop and could eavesdrop.

Emerging onto the sidewalk, he made eye contact with the guards. Angus gave him a thumbs-up.

"Look, Mommy, a fountain." Lily pointed to the park-like square across the street. "Can we go see it?"

The square was bustling with folks congregating on benches, enjoying donuts and coffee, and others walking their dogs along the brick paths. To the left and right of the Mint Julep Boutique, tourists and locals strolled along the sidewalks, their purchases swinging at their sides. It was a normal scene on a day with lovely weather. He looked at the beautiful woman beside him and wished the three of them could explore like a regular family. But the threat hadn't gone away.

"I'll bring you here again, I promise. For now, we should return to the cabin."

Lily started to pout. Tessa said, "We can ask Mimi if she wants to come over and swim. What do you think about that?"

"Okay."

Tessa locked gazes with him. "You didn't buy yourself anything."

"I'll stop in a store down the road. Won't take me five minutes to get what I need."

He made arrangements with Tyson and Angus, and

they followed closely during the brief drive to the Village Tinker. Tessa's eyebrows lifted. "This is where you're getting clothes?"

"I'm not difficult to please." He winked.

Inside, he breezed through the clothing section, snagging the bare necessities, then hurried to the real reason he'd come here. Back in the truck, he produced a large white box. Tessa wet her lips.

"Is that what I think it is?"

Lily leaned forward, only to be snagged by her booster-seat belt. "Can I see?"

"Lily, your mom and I used to come to this very store and buy their homemade fudge."

He opened the lid with a flourish, and the scents of rich, buttery caramel and chocolate filled the cab. Lily's eyes got huge as they took in the confectionary slabs.

Tessa immediately reached for her favorite, butter pecan. Her eyes closed in bliss as she tasted the first bite. "This hasn't changed a bit. Sweet perfection."

Mason chuckled. "Not as perfect as rocky road."

He handed Lily a piece of both. "Next time, I'll take you inside and let you choose a flavor."

In the middle of enjoying a second piece of fudge, his phone chirped. Tessa's enjoyment faded as he read the text.

"The tip didn't pan out," he told her, mourning the dip in her mood. Her gaze darted to the store and parking lot.

Mason tucked the purchases on the seat between them and put the gear in Reverse. Dante wasn't in the Bear Ridge neighborhood, as suspected, which meant he could be anywhere.

NINETEEN

Despite Mason's misgivings about the unit's involvement in the community outreach event, Lieutenant Hatmaker's stance didn't alter. They couldn't bow out. Mason and the others debated whether to leave Tessa and Lily at the cabin with the private security guards, Tyson and Angus, or to keep them with them. Because of the distance between Serenity and the neighboring city of Pigeon Forge, they decided on the latter.

Tyson and Angus had commandeered one of the stadium locker rooms for their use, and that's where she, Lily, Gia and Candace were supposed to stay until the community event was over. Restless and dogged by worry, Tessa had paced the smelly, oppressive room until Angus had had enough. He'd offered to accompany her for a quick peek at the mounted-police unit, to put her mind at ease, he'd gruffly said.

She remained in the cool shade created by the bleachers rising above her on either side. Behind her, a long tunnel led to the interior restrooms and snack bar. Angus stood slightly behind her shoulder, ready to shield her at any hint of trouble. As much as she disliked Lieutenant Hatmaker's attitude toward Mason, she had to agree with his assessment of today's threat level. Dante was arrogant, but he wasn't stupid. Even he would have second thoughts about trying something in the midst of this law-enforcement extravaganza.

The bleachers on this side of the high-school football field were mostly empty, as the event attendees were busy roaming the turf and drifting from one organization to the next. Students and faculty were joined by hundreds of citizens of all ages who'd come to learn about and interact with law enforcement and emergency services. Children got their pictures taken in shiny fire trucks. EMTs let volunteers practice wrapping and stabilizing pretend broken bones. The SWAT armored vehicle was obviously a crowd favorite.

The biggest draw of the day, though, was the mounted-police unit. The foursome and their respective mounts were mere yards away from this access point, and they were an impressive sight in their official Serenity PD gear. The equine officers' manes were in elevated, elegant braids along the crests of their necks. Their navy-and-silver saddle pads bore the department symbol and their individual names. Reflective breast-collar covers and leg wraps glinted when struck by the sun's rays.

Raven and Cruz interacted with attendees from their saddles, their two-toned helmets matching the saddle-pad colors. Silver and Mason stood with their horses and handed out bio cards. Due to his healing ribs, Mason had chosen not to get into the saddle. The fact that he was required to be here at all bothered Tessa. While he'd come to breakfast that morning looking rested, he hadn't been able to completely hide his discomfort. He'd reassured her he was recuperating nicely, and she had no choice but to believe him.

Watching him now, handsome and debonair in that blue-black uniform, mirrored shades and tall boots, she prayed for God's protection to continue. He had experienced tremendous losses since her return, both in material goods and his health. Yet he hadn't blamed her. Hadn't descended into self-pity. He'd focused all his energy on keeping her and Lily safe. She would've fallen for him if she hadn't loved him already.

"Time to return to the lair," Angus said.

"Can we swing by the snack bar on the way? It's almost suppertime."

Angus agreed. Tessa splurged on pizza, nachos and other not-so-healthy snacks, enough to share with everyone. Gia and Candace's lively personalities made the evening bearable. They doted on Lily, and she soaked in the attention like a thirsty forest lapping up a spring shower. Their two-member family had grown with their dash to Tennessee, and both Tessa and Lily had benefited.

It was growing late when Mason strode through the door and told them the event was winding down. His bruises had deepened to a dusky purple. The swelling had gone down, however. After quickly downing two slices of pizza, he hugged his mom and sister goodbye. Gia's vehicle was parked in a different area, and the pair would not be accompanying them to the stables.

Holding hands, Mason and Lily preceded Tessa onto the field. Tyson walked beside her, while Angus brought up the rear. Silver was waiting for them. He stood between Scout and Lightning and had both horses' leads. At the far end of the field, Raven and Cruz were riding their mounts into the grassy section where the unit trucks and trailers were parked.

Their group joined the mass exodus as attendees headed for their cars. Law-enforcement agencies were packing up their tables and tents. A handful of food vendors were also clearing out. When they reached the trucks, Mason immediately buckled Lily into her seat and urged Tessa to get in.

"Is something wrong?" she asked.

"No, I just don't want to take any chances." His gaze was hidden behind the sunglasses. "I'll be back as soon I help them get the horses settled."

The hired guards paced around the truck and didn't enter their own vehicle until Mason was behind the truck's wheel. They pulled into the departing traffic first, followed by Mason, and then in the second truck, Raven, Cruz and Silver.

The trip over had taken roughly forty-five minutes. Due to the volume of traffic surrounding the school, Tessa settled in for a longer return route, content to listen as Mason recounted the event highlights.

"I'm sorry you had to miss it," he said finally, glancing over.

"Who knows? Maybe I'll get to go next year."

"I'd like that." He wiped his forehead with his sleeve and adjusted the air vent. "You and I haven't had a chance to make plans or even discuss our options."

Options? Like an apartment for her somewhere in town, convenient to his home and work? She watched the stream of people navigating the metal-and-chrome sea. The school's flag waved gently in the breeze. The setting sun reflected in her side mirror, and she got her sunglasses from her cross-body bag.

Would she be successful at building a new life in Serenity like she had in Georgia? Could she handle living in the same town with Mason, loving him from afar and watching as one day he wooed and won someone else's heart?

Tessa forced her mind from the morose thoughts. What

good would come of thinking about a future when her present was balanced on a knife's edge?

When she didn't respond, Mason let the matter drop. Lily began humming as they entered Wears Valley Road, a sure sign she'd be asleep before they reached the stables. As they neared the dilapidated buildings and old water-park sign, Tessa's stomach cramped.

Mason sensed her distress and, reaching out, closed his hand over hers. "The memories won't ever go away. They'll lose their potency, though."

"I hope you're right, because I feel sick every time I picture them carrying you unconscious through the park and stowing you in the trunk."

A tortured look stole over his face. "Trust me, I get it. I would erase those images for you if I could."

She squeezed his hand. "I know."

As expected, Lily was asleep when they pulled into the stables' lot and parked. Tessa suggested staying inside the truck with her, but Mason shot down that idea. They had to unload the horses, remove their gear and brush them down, not to mention dole out their overdue supper.

Tessa carried her inside and got comfortable in one of the break-room chairs. She would've liked to help the officers, but they had a certain routine and would accomplish that faster without her underfoot. Fishing her phone from her pants pocket, she settled in to watch her favorite music videos.

At first, she didn't pay attention to the loud voices coming from deeper in the building. Then, a shot rang out, and she flinched. The door was flung open, and Mason filled the doorway, his jaw tight and his eyes hard.

"Dante's men are out there, and they're spraying the building with gasoline. They're going to burn us out and pick us off, one by one."

* * *

His cunning enemy had chosen to act when the bulk of law enforcement was in another town, packing up from the event or driving the twisting, winding connector road they'd taken. His unit had contacted dispatch. That didn't guarantee help would arrive before their stables were burned to the ground, just like his home.

"What's the plan?" Tessa asked, hurrying after him into the building's central area and shifting Lily's slumbering weight higher on her shoulder.

"You're riding into the mountains," Cruz answered for him. He'd led Iggy into the aisle and was putting a saddle on her.

Thankfully, they'd gotten the horses unloaded and inside before Dante's crew descended. Now, they had to find a way to save them.

Tessa stopped short of bumping into Mason. "Is that true?"

Again, someone else interjected. "It's your best option." Raven was stuffing water bottles and snacks into a backpack. "You'll exit through the rear door, which he won't be expecting, and ride through the trees until you can cross the road into wooded terrain. From there, you can skirt neighborhoods and keep out of sight. He would have a tough time pursuing you, even if he somehow spotted you."

From the side paddock entrance, he heard a distinct pop, followed by return fire. Tyson and Angus were out there trying to take out the goons with the hoses.

Mason was torn between the desire to stay and defend his unit, and getting Tessa and Lily out of harm's way. Part of being a good leader was learning when to delegate responsibility. Silver and the others would do everything within their power to prevent loss of life and damage to the facility. There was only one choice to be made.

"We'll need a sat phone." After retrieving one from the office, he joined Silver beside Scout's stall and stuffed it into his saddle pack.

"He could track your location with that."

"I'll keep it turned off unless there's an emergency." Mason strode to the weapons closet, used his key to unlock it and retrieved a rifle and ammo to go along with his pistol.

Cruz coaxed Iggy through the rear door. Mason looped his rifle sling over his head and, after motioning for Tessa to follow him, led Scout outside. This was a rarely used exit, and the strip of ground behind the building was uneven and overgrown.

Tessa coughed in reaction to the wall of gasoline fumes. Silver eased Lily from her arms so that she could climb onto Iggy's back. Raven rushed out and stuffed the snack supply inside his saddlebag. She held up a blanket.

"Found this in my locker. Use it to create a child wrap once you're far enough away. It'll make travel easier." After zipping up the bag, she hurried back inside. Cruz wasn't far behind.

"I'm going to head for the abandoned campground, Camp Smoky," Mason told Silver. "We can rendezvous there tomorrow morning."

"Good plan."

"Stay safe."

"Back at you."

Once Mason was astride Scout, he caught Tessa's gaze. "You ready?"

"I am."

He was grateful she was an experienced rider, because this wasn't going to be a fun trip. They were heading into residential areas fraught with unknown factors. At least his horses were trained to work through the unexpected.

They picked their way through the overgrowth of ferns and other greenery. At the point where the woods met the two-lane road, he waited for an opening in traffic before signaling to Tessa. A diagonal approach to the opposite lot led them through high grass and to another copse. They rarely conversed during their journey. Mason had to stay alert to potential pitfalls, and Tessa was concentrating on guiding her horse while keeping a snug hold on Lily. He would've liked to give her a break, but he had to be ready to fire a weapon at any moment.

When they encountered a group of tweens and teens kicking a soccer ball in a dense neighborhood, Mason urged Scout to keep riding. It wasn't their usual habit to ignore or avoid people in their community, and his equine partner was confused. But he followed Mason's directives and continued deeper into uninhabited territory.

The sun dipped behind the mountain ridge above them, cloaking the forest in a hazy shroud. Lily's distressed voice shredded the stillness, and Mason tugged on the reins and waited for Tessa and Iggy to come alongside.

He could barely make out their features, and the small clearing they were in was a blend of indistinct shapes.

Tessa rubbed Lily's tummy and murmured reassurances.

"I want to go home." She was trying to twist around and face Tessa. No wonder she was frightened, waking up to find herself far above the ground, balanced on a large animal. In the dark forest, no less.

"I know, ladybug, but Scout and Iggy are taking us on an adventure. Your daddy's here with us, and he's going to make sure we get to our destination. We're going to spend the night in a campground."

Lily clutched her mom's shirt. "I'm hungry."

"Raven packed us some snacks," Mason said, dismounting and using his flashlight to check the options in the backpack she'd tucked into his saddlebag. He wished he'd brought his pain meds, but quickly dismissed the thought. His mind needed to be sharp and clear. "Animal crackers or cheese squares? Or would you like a granola bar?"

"'Nola bar."

He removed the wrapper and handed it to her. While she ate, he gave Tessa a bottle of water and snagged one for himself.

"How are you?" he softly asked.

"Not too shabby." She shifted in the saddle and took another long drink. "You must be hurting."

"It's manageable."

"I guess it wouldn't be wise to use the sat phone and check on things?"

"Unfortunately, no." He couldn't stop thinking about his officers, human and equine, and wondering how they were faring. "If my calculations are correct, we should reach the camp in another hour."

Before she could respond, the sounds of revving engines, like angry bees, rocketed over the high crest above. Dirt bikes zoomed straight for the clearing. The bikes' lights flashed over them, temporarily blinding them and startling the horses.

Mason couldn't make out distinguishing features, body shapes or sizes. Were these joyriders out for an adrenaline rush, or were they locals hired to do Dante's bidding?

TWENTY

Tessa could feel Lily slipping from her grasp. Mason reached over and seized Iggy's reins, holding the horse steady as the trio of dirt bikes hurtled past them and disappeared into the thickening darkness.

She wrapped her right arm around Lily's middle and tugged her close. Her little body was shivering, despite the warm temperature. "It's okay, sweetheart. They're gone."

Tessa's heart was racing. For a split second, she'd thought Dante and his men had tracked them somehow and rented special equipment to reach them. While they had probably determined she and Mason weren't at the stables, they had no way of knowing their destination.

When Mason was convinced that Lily and the horses had calmed enough to resume their journey, he removed something from his saddlebag, snapped it in half and handed the glowing orange stick to Lily.

"Hold on to that, okay?"

She waved it around, clearly enamored. Mason reclaimed his position in the saddle. Tessa gave Iggy free rein. Horses had excellent night vision, especially with the full moon and stars acting as night-lights.

The rest of the trip was uneventful. With Lily's hunger assuaged and a new plaything to occupy her, she was content to rest in the circle of Tessa's arms. Occasionally, an owl's repetitive call would filter through the trees. Openings in the canopy above revealed wedges of star-studded sky.

"See the lake?" Mason said over his shoulder.

The terrain had leveled off about a mile back, and Tessa scanned the horizon, her eyes catching on the shimmering, reflective surface straight ahead.

"The lake marks the entrance to Camp Smoky," he continued. "There are multiple cabins rimming it. Beyond those are the old gymnasium, cafeteria and larger boarding structures used for big groups."

"Where will we stay?"

"The cabins are in bad shape, but one of the larger dorms will probably work. The owner doesn't live in the state anymore. He pays someone to tend the grounds. Patrol comes up here on a routine basis to check for uninvited guests."

"Like us, you mean?"

"Not quite," he replied, a smile in his voice. "Unless you hid a spray-paint can in your pocket."

Remembering the water park's dilapidated state, she suppressed a shudder. "Is there electricity?"

"Unfortunately, no."

"Then we won't be able to see s-p-i-d-e-r-s or m-i-c-e."

Laughter rumbled in his chest. "That's the first time anyone has spelled something at me."

She smiled. "It's a fact of life with a toddler."

"Noted." The horses ambled past the lake and along a gravel drive. "I'll check out our sleeping quarters. It won't be the most comfortable night, but we can cling to hope that Silver will bring fresh pastries for breakfast."

Moonlight enabled her to make out the basic details

of the structures. The heart of Camp Smoky was laid out in a circular pattern, with a large, semiwooded area in the middle of a ring of buildings. The cafeteria was a long, low cabin with a porch running the length of it. A chapel anchored one end of the circle, while a building that Mason said used to house miniature golf rental equipment and a general store was at the other.

After passing the chapel, Mason halted before a tall structure and passed his flashlight over it. Set back from the gravel circle, the cement building was painted a drab color. A generous wooden, ground-level porch had two sets of stairs leading to the upstairs deck.

"Why are there so many doors?"

"The dorm is separated into four sections on the first floor, to be used by different groups. There's a shared restroom with showers and toilets in the rear of the building. Upstairs, there's a maze of separate quarters."

Woods created a mysterious backdrop behind the buildings on this side of the camp. She tried to imagine children spending happy summer days here and couldn't quite manage it.

They dismounted and tethered the horses to the post-and-rail fence. She and Lily waited on the porch while Mason tested windows. He found one that was unlocked, slid it open and climbed inside. She could see his light move through the space. Seconds later, the door swung open.

"Would you believe there are still mattresses in the bunks?"

"How long has this been closed to campers?" She entered the tight space and surveyed the floor-to-ceiling wooden bunks, three beds high.

Mason got on his knees and searched the slots underneath. When he didn't spy any critters, he began shaking out the thin blue mattresses.

"I'm not sure exactly. Two years. Maybe three."

They ate by aid of an upturned flashlight. Afterward, Mason urged her to get some sleep while he kept watch outside. Lily clambered onto one of the lowest bunks and clutched her orange glow stick.

"Watch this, ladybug." Wrappers crinkled. Plastic snapped. In a matter of seconds, he'd placed glow sticks around the room. Yellow, blue, orange, red. They created a fluorescent display that dispelled the grim atmosphere.

She giggled and sighed into her arms, which she was using as a makeshift pillow. "Pretty, Daddy."

Tessa snagged his hand, pulled him close and hugged him. He hesitated, then lightly ran his hand over her hair before cupping her nape. The weight of his palm was warm and familiar.

He hadn't had a chance to change out of his uniform, and the starched fabric was pulled taut over his bullet-proof vest.

"What's this for?" he murmured.

"You're amazing, that's all."

"Because of glow sticks?" he asked good-naturedly. "If I'd known how easy it was to impress you, I would've brought those out days ago."

Tessa forced her arms to release him. Going forward, she couldn't give in to random hugs and spontaneous shows of affection. Their dire circumstances had forged a new bond between them. She was certain he felt it, too—this renewed sense of solidarity and the knowledge they could depend on each other. The broken trust had been repaired.

Her love for him refused to be confined to the deepest, most hidden part of herself. Tessa understood what that meant for her—a life of longing for something she could never have, a life of loneliness and heartache. No other man could take his place.

Tessa would do what was best for Mason and their daughter. Over time, she would come to accept that her role in his life was that of a co-parent and friend, nothing more.

"You're a wonderful, thoughtful father, Mason." Emotion leaked into her voice.

His rugged features were encased in multicolored light, allowing her to see his shy smile. "Thank you, Tess. That means a lot coming from you. You make parenting look easy."

"I've had practice. You, on the other hand, know instinctively what to do. Glow sticks don't impress me. You do."

He rocked back on his heels. Before she added to her sentimental confession, she found a spot beside Lily.

"Sweet dreams." His voice was a soft caress.

She closed her eyes and ordered the wishes and dreams inside her to die a swift death.

He checked his cell phone throughout the night. Every time, he was met with a no-service message. The temptation to turn on the sat phone was great.

Were the stables intact? The horses safe? His officers unharmed? Had Dante slipped through their grasp once again?

The continuous loop of his thoughts returned to Tessa. So much had changed since she'd stormed back into his life. He would do anything for her, including taking a bullet for her. That had been true four years ago, and it was true today.

He walked along the platform that linked the building

to the gravel drive and greeted Scout and Iggy. Across the grassy expanse, faded neon lights could be seen through the window of the girls' room. Was Tessa asleep? If not, was she thinking about him? About her and him together?

Absently rubbing his aching side, he studied the sky transforming from deep navy to shimmery lilac. She hadn't indicated in the slightest that she wanted a do-over with him. All she wanted was his forgiveness and his promise they would raise Lily as a cohesive team. He was fine with that. Perfectly satisfied.

They couldn't re-create what they used to have. To think they could was arrogant and foolish.

Why, then, did the thought of living on the fringes of her life make him want to put his fist through a wall?

Mason's mind refused to rest as dawn broke. His gaze strayed often to the gravel drive in anticipation of Silver's promised arrival. But his friend didn't show, and the sun climbed ever higher. Lily emerged from the room shortly after eight o'clock. Bright-eyed and bursting with energy, she skipped through the grass and wrapped her arms around his legs.

"Morning, ladybug." He smoothed her curls. Gazing into her precious face, he again thanked God for the opportunity to be a father. "How did you sleep?"

"Mommy said I had a dream about a ship."

Tessa joined them, her smile edged with fatigue. "She rolled and thrashed as if she were on a ship's deck."

She pulled her hair into a ponytail and applied a fresh layer of lip balm. "No sign of Silver?"

"Not yet." He stood as Lily bounced away.

Her hazel gaze swept him from head to toe. "Why don't you lie down for a while? I'll let Lily stretch her legs and keep an eye out for him."

It was a tempting offer, especially since he hadn't gotten his usual boost of caffeine. "If I go to sleep now, you may never pry me from the bunk. He should be here soon."

Unless things had gone south...

"Hey." She touched his arm, righting his focus. "I'm worried, too, but we can't lose faith."

"Mommy, I gotta go potty." Lily danced around Tessa.

"Let's go in those trees over there."

While Tessa was taking care of things with Lily, Mason opened a new bottle of water, chugged half the contents and splashed the rest over his face. A sudden flurry of birds exiting the woods near the cafeteria had him reaching for his pistol.

Seconds later, the report of a rifle echoed through the camp and a high-velocity bullet hurtled straight for him. He dove to the ground as the fence railing above him exploded in a shower of splinters.

He saw Tessa and Lily walking back, oblivious to the danger. One of the building's stairways stood between them.

"Get inside!" he yelled.

Another shot dug into the dirt near his boots, and he crawled away from the girls. Like he had during the river incident, he would draw the enemy in a different direction. How Dante had located them was a troubling mystery.

He heard Lily's plaintive cry as Tessa scooped her up and pounded across the porch to safety. As soon as the door slammed shut, he continued his fast crawl through the grass. When he reached gravel, he got to his feet and sprinted for the octagonal ball pit on the far side of the lane, then leaped over the knee-high panels. Hitting the cement, he used the panels for cover as he surveyed the woods beyond the basketball court.

The crunch of tires on gravel distracted him. The familiar logo painted on the truck and trailer penetrated his adrenaline high, and he offered up a prayer of thanks.

He signaled to get Silver's attention. The truck came under fire, so Silver stopped and opened his door. Raven was in the passenger seat. From this angle, he could see her prepping her service weapon and speaking into her radio.

Mason's yell reached him, and Silver acknowledged the warning. There was a blur of movement in the woods. A man who looked like James left the trees, skirted the basketball courts and disappeared behind another dorm. He couldn't be allowed to escape. His route would circle around the dorm, volleyball court and chapel, leading him to the dorm where Tessa and Lily were hiding.

Silver pursued the mustached man. Mason left the ball pit and returned to their dorm. No one answered his summons, so he kicked down the door and strode through the room, calling for Tessa.

The bathroom stalls were vacant. He walked down the line of showers, yanking open the curtain dividers one by one, his heart sinking like a stone when he failed to find them and there was no response to his calls.

"Mason?"

He whirled, expecting to see Tessa. In his rising panic, he'd mistaken the owner of the voice.

Raven stood beside the sinks in full gear, her weapon ready and her expression a mixture of fierce determination and compassion.

"They're not here," he rasped.

Dante had gotten to them. He'd taken the two people on this planet that he couldn't live without. His lungs squeezed, and he felt like he was going to suffocate.

"I lost the love of my life," she said. "I won't let that happen to you." Stalking to the exit door, she ripped it open. "Let's go get them back."

TWENTY-ONE

"Cat got your tongue, sis?"

Tessa didn't waste her breath begging for mercy. Tenderness and compassion had been drilled out of her brother. She held Lily close and sent her desperate pleas to God.

They'd left the dorm behind and, with Bruno bringing up the rear, marched beneath the shade trees that separated the dorm and chapel. A Suburban was parked near the chapel's rear exit and rusted air-conditioning unit. There were three of them here—Dante, Bruno and a third man tasked with killing Mason. What did that mean for the mounted police officers?

"What happened last night? Did you burn down the stables?"

Dante's answer was a scowl and flaring of his nostrils, which gave her hope. Maybe the fire department had arrived in time. Maybe the others had defended their headquarters until Dante and his crew had been forced to give up.

"How did you find us?"

"Social media can be a useful tool. You and Sergeant Reed captured the attention of a group of kids playing soccer. They took photos and posted them online. We got a map of the area and checked several places before coming here." He leaned in and spoke to Lily. His signature citrusy cologne enveloped them. "I'm your Uncle Dante. Do you remember me talking to you through your video system in Georgia?"

Lily's arms tightened around her neck. Tessa would've put distance between them, but Bruno was behind her, a large gun pointed at her spine. The humidity and intensifying heat from the sun weren't responsible for the sweat popping up on her skin. She was trying not to reveal her terror to her daughter, but it was growing more difficult by the minute.

"I heard you like horses. I have lots of horses at my home in New Jersey, and I'm going to take you to see them. You can learn to ride. Your Aunt Francesca also loves horses and will be your teacher. What do you think about that?"

When Lily didn't respond, he touched her shoulder. Tessa flinched. Fire ignited in his eyes, and he held out his arms.

"Give her to me."

Tessa shook her head. Her insides were quaking. This couldn't be the outcome. Dante couldn't win.

"Don't make this difficult for her," he growled. He wasn't thinking of her, though. He was worried about having to handle a toddler-sized meltdown.

Tessa glanced around. The chapel blocked her view of the wooded recreational area in the middle of the inner circle. There was no sign of Mason. Was he unconscious somewhere, felled by a bullet?

Would this abandoned campground be her final resting place?

She took a trembling breath. "Ladybug, I want you to go with Uncle Dante for a little while."

Lily burrowed closer. Tessa smoothed her hair and kissed the top of her head.

"I love you, Lily."

"Enough." Dante rolled his eyes and took her daughter from her.

Her heart shattered as Lily arched her body to try and reach Tessa.

"Calm down," Dante commanded. He opened the rear door while trying to corral Lily. "Why don't you sit in here—"

"Daddy!"

Dante spun around and Lily wiggled free. She ran to Mason, her short legs pumping with all their might. He had left the cover of the trees between the dorm and chapel, his rifle trained on Dante.

Time slowed. Tessa's frantic mind couldn't decide between fight or flight. Just as Lily reached Mason, Raven strode out of the trees. Holstering her pistol, she caught the toddler and hustled her along the chapel's long exterior.

Dante lunged for Tessa and shoved a gun to her temple. "Now we have a problem."

Mason's stance didn't falter. "There's a simple solution." He held the rifle steady, and his body was locked into offensive mode. "Free Tessa and turn yourself in."

Bruno inched closer to his boss. "What's the plan?"

Speaking loudly enough for Mason to hear, he said, "Tessa is my ticket out of here. I'm not giving her to you." His fingers dug into her upper arm, and she whimpered. "I'm going to do what I should've done long ago—rid the Vitale family of its black sheep. Mark my words, Sergeant Reed, I'll be back for my niece. Next time, you won't see me coming."

Mason's gaze didn't stray to her once. His expression remained shuttered. How could he be so calm?

"I can't let you leave, Dante. You're going to serve time for your crimes."

Dante began to laugh his cruel, self-satisfied laugh, the one that instilled fear in her, the one that signaled he'd won.

There was a sharp report, and his laughter was cut off. He grunted and fell to his knees. A second gunshot, this one much closer, hit Bruno. The large man slumped against the Suburban and would've fired at Mason if he hadn't received another bullet in the arm.

Mason and Silver descended on the injured men and gathered up their weapons, then flipped them on their stomachs and slapped on restraints.

Through it all, Tessa stood immobile, afraid to move or even breathe. Was the danger truly over?

"James?" Mason barked at Silver.

Breathing heavily, his gray hair sliding into his eyes, he gave a thumbs-up sign. "Trussed up like a Christmas goose."

"Where's the fourth one? Baldy?"

"In the county jail. Snagged him last night before the others bolted," Silver replied. "We didn't suffer any losses."

Mason's gaze found Tessa. The almost predatory fierceness in the brown depths slowly faded as he acknowledged she was unharmed.

"Is it over?" she whispered.

His throat convulsed. "It's over."

Dante thrashed and spewed threats, reclaiming Mason's attention.

"I'm going to find Raven and Lily," Tessa told him.

She needed to be far away from her deranged brother. More than that, she needed to be with her daughter.

He merely nodded, effectively dismissing her. Tessa understood that he had to be in police mode right now, but she craved his reassuring embrace. She'd almost lost Lily forever. She'd had a gun shoved at her head. She'd stood between two men who'd been taken down by officers.

She wanted his arms around her and his reassurances that everything would be okay, that their renewed friendship would remain strong. She wanted much more than that, but wanting more made her feel greedy.

Mason had forgiven her and had let her back into his life. Wasn't that enough?

As she reunited with Raven and Lily, her mind turned to the future. How long would Silver let her and Lily stay in the cabin? Where would Mason stay? Would he expect her to leave Lily with him while she retrieved her belongings from Georgia?

Would he expect to have a say in where she and Lily lived? Would he put in a good word for her wherever she applied for a job?

As soon as backup arrived, Raven drove them to the cabin, where Gia awaited. While Lily greeted her grandmother, the officer took Tessa aside.

"Want my advice? Eat something, take a long bubble bath and try to relax. Mason will be tied up for a while."

She took a deep breath and nodded. Her pulse wouldn't settle, despite the knowledge they weren't in danger anymore.

"Thank you again for everything."

Her gaze turned assessing. "You don't look relieved."

"I am."

Raven obviously wasn't convinced. "You and Mason will figure things out. Don't waste the second chance you've been given." Her smile was sad. "Not everyone gets a second chance."

With that, she climbed into the vehicle and left. Tessa spent part of the morning doing as Raven had suggested, indulging in a full breakfast prepared by Gia and taking a restorative bath in the luxurious master suite. They had lunch on the covered deck overlooking the mountain ridges dancing into the horizon. By midafternoon, she was wondering if Mason even planned on returning to the cabin. When Gia offered to put Lily down for a nap, Tessa gratefully accepted. She took a stack of magazines from the living room out to the deck and got comfortable on the bench.

Sometime later, the glass door slid open and Mason emerged.

"Mason."

Tessa jumped up, not caring about the magazine fluttering to her feet. Judging by his clean clothes and freshly washed hair, he'd been here long enough to shower and change. Or maybe he'd done that at the stables, which, Raven had informed her, had not suffered any damage. Fire crews and a sheriff's deputy had arrived in time to save the day.

He closed the door and strode toward her with purpose. He was wearing yellow again, one of her favorite colors on him because it paired perfectly with his tan skin, and dark hair and eyes. As usual, his handsome, rugged appearance had a devastating effect on her equilibrium. How was she supposed to pretend that friendship would satisfy her?

"I didn't hear you arrive—"

He framed her face with his calloused hands and brought his mouth down on hers, stealing her words and wiping rational thought from her mind.

Tessa wrapped her arms around his waist and locked her hands behind him, both to keep him close and to maintain her balance. His lips were firm and searching, his fingertips gentle as they slid into her hair and cupped her head. It had always been like this between them—instant connection, a heady combination of emotion and attraction. Mason was her normal, her safety net, her family.

Beneath her hands, his back muscles quivered. He lifted his head and gazed at her with hope-brightened eyes. "I still love you, Tess."

Happiness bloomed inside her, chasing away the darkness of the past four years.

"Oh, Mason, I never stopped loving you," she whispered, her smile stretching from ear to ear.

His mouth curved into a dazzling, teeth-flashing smile that weakened her knees. He was looking at her with unabashed love and acceptance, not like before. *Better* than before. There were no more secrets between them. Mason knew the true her, Tessa Lenore Vitale.

He removed something from his pocket and, swallowing hard, placed it in the palm of her hand. "I bought this for you a week before things blew up in our faces."

Tessa stared at the tiny velvet bag. "You kept it all this time?"

"I couldn't bring myself to part with it."

Her fingers trembling, she removed the hard, round object and blinked at the gold band topped with a shiny diamond.

"It's lovely."

He took her hand and went down on one knee. "You're the only woman I've ever wanted for my wife," he said gruffly. "What do you say, Tess? Will you give us another chance? Will you marry me?"

"I say try and stop me!" As soon as he slid the ring into place, she threw her arms around his neck and kissed him.

When she lifted her head, he grinned and got to his feet. "We've got a lot to do before we can get married. Clear out your house in Georgia—"

"I'd like to explain things to Lisa and my other friends and say goodbye. Lily will want to attend story hour one last time."

"Of course. There's also the small matter of rebuilding the house."

That would take months, she realized with dismay. Possibly a year or more.

"I've waited this long to be with you," she finally said. "I can be patient."

"I'm not sure I can," he announced, trailing his fingers along her cheek. "I'm ready for the three of us to be a family."

Anticipation danced along her skin. "I don't care where we live, as long as we're together."

He laughed. "Even a tent?"

"Even a tent."

She kissed him again, thanking God for His mercy and grace. With Him as their foundation, they could look forward to a union built on faith and love.

EPILOGUE

"You may kiss the bride."

Mason brushed a lingering kiss on Tessa's smiling mouth. He'd been waiting a lifetime for this moment. The small assembly of guests clapped and cheered, and he could hear Silver whistling nearby.

He lifted his head, caressed her cheek and smiled into her shining, gold-and-green eyes. "Have I told you how stunning you are, Mrs. Reed?"

Pink tinged her cheeks. The top section of her hair had been twisted into place, paper-thin white and pink flowers tucked among the shiny strands, and the remaining curls cascaded past her shoulders. The simple, elegant cut of her dress showed off her smooth shoulders, toned arms and slender waist. Round diamond studs winked at her ears.

She ran her hand down his tuxedo lapel. "Have I told you this tuxedo isn't going back to the rental store, Mr. Reed?"

"What would I need a tuxedo for?"

Tessa adopted an innocent expression. "To wear to Silver's wedding, of course."

His best man's face flushed red, and he appeared to choke. A laughing Cruz pounded him on the back.

Behind Tessa, Candace signaled him. "Are you two going to stand here all day chatting, or are you going to cut the cake?"

"Cut the cake!" Lily bounced on her toes, her beribboned dress flouncing around her ankles.

His mom, Raven and the other guests laughed as the remaining flower petals in her basket wound up on the floor.

Mason held out his arm, and Tessa slid her hand in the crook of his elbow. Together, they walked through the wedding chapel and into the May sunshine. He stopped on the porch and turned to his bride.

"I'm the most fortunate man in the world," he told her, cupping her cheek.

The danger had passed. Dante had been killed by a rival family while in police custody. Bruno, James and others in the Vitale employ were still awaiting trial. Tessa's father was too frail to continue the family business, and rumor was that the Vitale empire was quickly crumbling without anyone to take charge. Mason had asked if Tessa wanted to speak to her sister and mother, to try and reestablish a relationship without Dante around to poison it. She'd said she wasn't ready, and he hadn't pressed the issue.

Tessa leaned into him, her love for him written on her face. "I'll be forever grateful for second chances and new beginnings."

Mason had thought they couldn't re-create what they'd had in the past. He'd been right. They had to let go of the past in order to start anew. Together, he, Tessa and Lily would build a different life—a better, brighter life—as a family who loved and trusted God, above all else.

"Me, too, sweetheart. Me, too." He pulled her into his arms and kissed her again.

* * * * *

If you enjoyed this book, look for these other suspense stories by Karen Kirst:

Danger in the Deep
Intensive Care Crisis
Forgotten Secrets

Dear Reader,

I'm thrilled you chose to join me on this new adventure with the Serenity Mounted Police Unit. I am happy to be writing about East Tennessee and the incomparable Great Smoky Mountains National Park again. I was born and raised in this area and know how much locals and visitors adore this place. I'm looking forward to writing the other officers' stories, and I hope you're eager to read them.

There are two actual mounted-police units in Tennessee, and I was extremely fortunate to connect with one police sergeant who patiently and thoroughly answered my many questions. I owe him a huge debt of thanks, because this series wouldn't be possible without his input. Obviously, any mistakes in situations or procedures are my own.

You can learn more about my historical and suspense books on my website, www.karenkirst.com. I'm active on Facebook, or you can reach out via email, karenkirst@live.com.

Blessings,
Karen Kirst

COMING NEXT MONTH FROM
Love Inspired Suspense

Available May 11, 2021

WILDERNESS DEFENDER
Alaska K-9 Unit • by Maggie K. Black
When ruthless poachers target rare blue bear cubs, K-9 trooper Poppy Walsh and her Irish wolfhound, Stormy, will do whatever it takes to stop them. But having to work with her ex-fiancé, park ranger Lex Fielding, will be her biggest test. Can they overcome their past to save the cubs and protect Lex's toddler son?

EVIDENCE OF INNOCENCE
by Shirlee McCoy
Determined to find her father's true killer when she's finally exonerated and freed after seventeen years in prison, Kinsley Garrett puts herself right into a murderer's crosshairs. But with help from her neighbor, police chief Marcus Bayne, can she survive long enough to expose the truth?

AMISH COUNTRY COVER-UP
by Alison Stone
When Amish nanny Liddie Miller is attacked more than once while caring for Jonah Troyer's children, the attempts stir up too many memories of his wife's murder for comfort. But with the police insisting her murderer died in prison, only Jonah can protect Liddie...and make sure the culprit is brought to justice.

TAKEN IN THE NIGHT
Mount Shasta Secrets • by Elizabeth Goddard
Danielle Collins has no idea how she and her daughter will escape the man who shot her brother—until her ex, Reece Bradley, comes to their rescue. Now on the run with the secret father of her child, Danielle must rely on Reece to figure out what someone wants from them...before it's too late.

COLD CASE TRAIL
by Sharee Stover
Ten years after her best friend's unsolved murder, forensic psychologist Justine Stark discovers a diary that could blow the case open—and she becomes a target. With Nebraska state trooper Trey Jackson and his K-9 partner, Magnum, at her side, can she finally catch the killer determined to silence her?

TEXAS RANCH SABOTAGE
by Liz Shoaf
Someone's dead set on sabotaging Tempe Calloway's ranch, no matter who they hurt in the process. Special agent Ewen Duncan doesn't trust Tempe, but he's sure the attacks have something to do with why the single mother took something from his home in Scotland. And he'll risk everything to keep her safe...and uncover her secrets.

SPECIAL EXCERPT FROM

LOVE INSPIRED SUSPENSE
INSPIRATIONAL ROMANCE

A K-9 trooper must work with her ex to bring down a poaching ring in Alaska.

Read on for a sneak preview of
Wilderness Defender *by Maggie K. Black,*
the next book in the Alaska K-9 Unit series,
available May 2021 from Love Inspired Suspense.

Lex Fielding drove, cutting down the narrow dirt path between the towering trees. Branches slapped the side of his park-ranger truck, and rocks spun beneath his wheels. All the while, words cascaded through his mind, clattering and colliding in a mass of disjointed ideas that didn't even begin to come close to what he wanted to say to Poppy. Years ago, he'd had no clue how to explain to the most incredible woman he'd ever known that he didn't think he was ready to get married and have a family. He might not have even had the guts to tell her all his doubts, if she hadn't called him out on it after he'd left a really unfortunate and accidental pocket-dial message on Poppy's voice mail admitting he wasn't ready to get married.

Something about being around Poppy had always made him feel like a better man than he had any right being. Even standing beside her made him feel an inch taller.

He just hadn't thought he'd been cut out to be anyone's husband. Something he'd then proved a couple of years later by marrying the wrong woman and surviving a couple of unhappy years together before she'd tragically died in a car crash.

He heard the chaos ahead before he could even see it through the thick forest. A dog was barking furiously, voices were shouting, and above it all was a loud and relentless banging sound, like something was trying to break down one of the cabins from the inside.

He whispered a prayer and asked God for wisdom. Hadn't been big on prayer outside of church on Sundays back when he'd been planning on marrying Poppy. But ever since Danny had been born, he'd been relying on it more and more to get through the day.

Then the trees parted, just in time for him to see the two figures directly in front of him dragging something across the road. His heart stopped.

Not something. *Someone.*

They had Poppy.

Don't miss
Wilderness Defender *by Maggie K. Black,*
available May 2021 wherever Love Inspired Suspense
books and ebooks are sold.

LoveInspired.com

LOVE INSPIRED

INSPIRATIONAL ROMANCE

UPLIFTING STORIES OF FAITH, FORGIVENESS AND HOPE.

———————————

Join our social communities to connect with other readers who share your love!

Sign up for the Love Inspired newsletter at **LoveInspired.com** to be the first to find out about upcoming titles, special promotions and exclusive content.

———————————

CONNECT WITH US AT:

Facebook.com/LoveInspiredBooks

Twitter.com/LoveInspiredBks

Facebook.com/groups/HarlequinConnection

LISOCIAL2020